Meant to Be

(The Saving Angels book 1)

By Tiffany King

www.authortiffanyjking.blogspot.com

To my wonderful husband, Karl.
None of this would have been possible without you.
And also to my beautiful children, Ashlynn and Ryan, for
being so patient throughout this journey.
I love you.

Chapter 1

The dream was as familiar as always, but that didn't keep my heart from practically beating out of my chest from the anticipation of seeing him again. The bright moonlight overhead and the lights from the amusement park in the distance provided just enough light to see him waiting for me. I couldn't help the smile that tugged at the corner of my mouth as I slowly walked toward him. The hard packed wet sand crunched under my bare feet as I walked along the tide line. I could feel the cold water lapping over the top of my feet, reaching my ankles. The fact that I have never seen his face didn't diminish the intimacy that has blossomed from the many nights we have spent together. There was a subtle, cool breeze off the ocean that might have chilled me if not for his warm embrace that comforted me like a down blanket on a cold winter night. I hoped against hope that the new twist of the dreams was a fluke, and that tonight would be different. I felt his fingers tighten around mine, and I tried with every bit of strength I had to hold on, but the invisible force yanked him away like a kite in the wind, and in an instant he was gone.

I woke to a damp pillow from the tears I had shed while dreaming.

The dream had changed over the last few weeks and I could hardly control the sorrow that filled me when I awakened. I didn't understand why, after dreaming about him my whole life, the dreams were now different. What was this mysterious force that suddenly pulled him away, leaving me all alone in the darkness?

I sat up and brushed away the wet blonde strands of hair that was stuck to the moisture on my face.

Glancing at the alarm clock beside my bed, I was dismayed to see that dawn was just minutes away, and my alarm would be going off any minute.

"Well, I might as well go take my shower now," I told Feline.

Feline was my cat, and even though he was getting up in cat years, and would rather stay on my comfortable bed, he peeked his eyes open at the sound of my voice. When he saw me watching, he closed his eyes back up and snuggled even deeper into the blankets.

For the first time that morning, I smiled. Even though he looked like he was zonked out, I knew he would beat me to the bathroom.

Sure enough, the instant I swung my legs over the edge of the bed, Feline was at my feet.

Bending over, I scratched him behind his ears before heading out of my room. With Feline at my heels, I walked down the hallway to the bathroom.

I was finally getting used to the set up of the new house and had stopped opening the hallway closet door to go to the bathroom. The first night, I actually walked all the way into the closet before realizing I wasn't in the bathroom. In my defense, I had been half asleep, but it was still embarrassing, especially after telling my mom. My mom teased me and said maybe we should put signs on the bathroom doors like you see in restaurants, if that would help.

I could feel the flush of embarrassment begin to creep up my neck as it headed for my face. I knew my mom didn't really think I would have used it as a bathroom, but it didn't take much to embarrass me. "Just joking sweetie," my mom had said, reaching over and patting my hand.

"I know." My red face couldn't hide my embarrassment.

If I could change one thing about myself, it would be the fact that everything made me blush. Most girls would want to change something about their appearance, but not me. Not that I think I'm anything great, as a matter fact, I pretty much feel I'm a lost cause.

If asked to describe myself, I would mumble medium height, blue eyes, dish water blonde hair, average build, and a chest not worth bragging about. There were so many ordinary aspects to my body that I was in the opinion you would have to change my whole palate to make me beautiful. No, if I could change anything, I would change the fact that my face flushed red at the drop of a hat. Everything seemed to tinge my cheeks with color. It didn't matter if someone paid me a compliment, or if a teacher called on me in class, everything made my face bright with color.

Often, even watching sitcoms was difficult for me. If I sensed something was going to embarrass a character on a show, I would have to flip the channel to avoid almost becoming sick from empathy. My dad used to lightly tease me about it when I was younger. He would call me their "sense-a-meter."

There was no denying that I was sensitive. If a book was sad, it was a given that I would cry buckets reading it. If a movie had a sad ending, I would walk around sad for days afterwards. My parents quickly learned to curb my movie watching and to keep all depressing movies away from me. They often joked that they were the only parents that had to keep their child away from Disney movies. When I was eight, it had taken me weeks to get over Bambi's mother dying. It wasn't just books and movies that I was sensitive to. I was also keenly aware of the emotions of other people around me. If my parents were happy, I was filled with a warm joyful feeling. To the other extreme though, if they were sad, I was filled with unexplainable grief.

Growing up, once my parents became aware of just how sensitive I was, they tried to mask their emotions to spare me the agony they felt I went through. This adjustment made life easier for me and for the most part I lived my life relatively happy. That is until a year ago when my dad died from a heart attack during his morning run; my world was shattered.

After his sudden death, I wound up spending a few weeks in the hospital. At first the doctors thought I was suffering from depression, but it was more deeply rooted. My own grief

4

compounded with my sensitivity to my mom's sorrow was almost enough to kill me. The doctors were flabbergasted that even sleeping pills did not seem to give me the peace I needed. They observed that if I fell into a natural sleep, I seemed more peaceful.

My dreams had always been the soothing medicine that I needed for any pain that I experienced in life. We have never once, in all our years together spoken a single word, but we share a conscious bond that makes it unnecessary.

For obvious reasons, I had to keep this info to myself since the doctor's already thought I was a basket case. I could just imagine what they would think if I told them I was comforted by some boy I had been dreaming about all my life, and even though he always stood in the shadows, and I had never seen his face clearly, I was in love with him. Not even my parents knew everything about the dreams. Sure, they knew that I occasionally dreamed about some boy I had never met, but I never let on that I dreamt of him every night, and that he is the reason I paid no attention to the boys in school.

My grief over my dad's passing gradually lifted, and I started to function again. I knew a big part of this was because my mom realized that I could not handle her grief on top of my own. She learned to hide her own grief when I was around. I felt bad that she had to mask her own sorrow, but I could not help appreciating the loosening of the band of sadness that had encircled me.

I knew my mom still missed my dad even a year later, and often at night I could still sometimes hear her crying in her room.

That's why we were in a new house, in a new town.

Two months ago after our first Christmas without my dad, my mom abruptly closed the book she had been reading at the breakfast table. At the slam of the book, I looked up startled from my own book.

"That's it," she had announced. "We're moving."

"What?" I asked, not sure I heard her right. "Moving?" We had lived in this house as long as I could remember.

"Were moving," she repeated.

"Why?"

"Because we are never going to let go of him if we stay in this town, everywhere we go reminds us of him. The movies, our favorite restaurants, even the mall. I'm reminded of him wherever I go, and I know you are too. We need a new beginning."

"Isn't moving expensive?" I asked, not sure my mom had thought this through completely. We weren't poor, but I knew that both my parents had to work to maintain their lifestyle. I had been worrying about how we were going to make ends meet since my dad had died.

"We have the money from your dad's life insurance."

"Dad had life insurance?" I asked surprised.

"Yes, we both had policies in our name. We took them out after we adopted you. We wanted to make sure if anything ever happened to us, you would be taken care of."

I felt the familiar pang in my heart. I knew I should get over being abandoned, but for some reason I could not let it go that my "real" parents didn't love me enough to keep me. I knew my adoptive parents loved me like I was their own flesh and blood, but I couldn't help wondering why I had been left behind by my real parents.

"How much money is the policy?" I had asked, shaking off the bothersome thoughts.

"Enough that you never have to worry about college and you get to spend your last couple months of school in private school."

I was thrilled. Attending a private school had been a lifelong dream of mine. Not because I was vain and wanted to surround myself with other smart kids, but because I felt if I attended a school where there were other kids with high IQ's, I could get lost in the crowd. Don't ask me why I had assumed everyone at private school were smart, I had just always perceived it that way.

In public school I always seemed to be the smartest in my class, and my teachers were always trying to get my parents to have my IQ tested, but I always fought it. I didn't want to skip grades. I didn't want to be tested for gifted classes. I just wanted to be like any other teenager. For years my goal was to fly under the radar. I always got straight A's, but I never went beyond that. The less attention I got, the happier I was.

It was easier when I had teachers that didn't care much about their jobs, and had only gone into teaching for the summers off. They appreciated kids like me who made their jobs easier. The teachers that actually liked their jobs were harder to fool. Usually, after a couple of months, they would catch on to just how smart I was and then the cycle would start over again. They would meet with my parents.

"Do you know Krista is gifted?" They would ask.

"Yes," my parents would reply.

"Would you like us to test her?"

"No," my parents would say. "We think Krista is comfortable where she is."

I had seen this cycle many times and just wanted to put it all behind me. I felt a private school was the way to go, but they were expensive and I knew that it would be too costly for me to attend one, so I had never asked.

"Yes," my mom replied.

"There's more, I've been researching private schools and guess where one of the best in the nation is located?"

"Santa Cruz?" I asked, not daring to believe my good fortune.

"Yep!" she replied, using one of my favorite slang words.

Except for being overly sensitive and dreaming about some guy I had never met, the next craziest thing about me was my ridiculous, burning desire to visit Santa Cruz. My parents could never explain this strange desire of mine, but I couldn't help wondering if I was born there or something like that.

The Department of Children and Family Services had no information to pass on about me, except the fact that some woman found me sitting on a park bench at a rest stop in Utah, when I was two. I was found clutching a bear and a small backpack. I couldn't tell them my name, and all the social workers could get out of me was that "Franklin," or what sounded like Franklin, had told me to sit until someone came to help me. The authorities searched the area high and low for anyone close to the name of Franklin, but their searches proved to be fruitless.

"Santa Cruz," I had repeated. Saying the name out loud filled me with an unexplainable rightness.

Now, two months later, here we were. From the moment we drove through the town limits, I had felt it. I didn't know why, but I knew I belonged here.

I studied my reflection in the mirror over the sink as I smoothed moisturizer on my face. The sea air was playing havoc on my complexion. I hated the constant gritty texture my face seemed to have and the dark black smudges under my eyes that made me resemble a NFL football player. I couldn't help feeling a little frazzled about starting school the next day. It was one thing to feel like a freak on the inside, but a whole other thing to look like one.

I traced the dark smudges with my fingertip. The gritty texture of my skin could be fixed, but the smudges would be harder to cover up. The dream had shaken me more than I was willing to admit. I was terrified at what they meant. Was he going to leave me after all these years? How would I function without him? Who would I turn to in my times of need?

All of these thoughts filled me with despair, and sleep was now a double edge sword. I longed to see him, but I feared for the day he would no longer be there.

I stepped into the shower after laying down an extra towel under the bathmat. The shower door was older, and no matter how hard we closed it, it still leaked around the edges.

Hoping the water would wash away the last lingering side effects from the dream, I deliberately twisted the knob to the hottest setting. Of course it took a while, since the hot water heater in the house must have been installed when the house was built twenty years ago. My mom told me that it couldn't be that old, since typically hot water heaters only lasted about ten years. It may not be twenty years old, but it had definitely seen better days, and was another item on the endless "to do" list hanging on the refrigerator. My mom and I aren't the handiest with tools, so the list keeps growing while nothing ever gets crossed off. My mom promised to call a handyman last night after the pantry door fell off its hinges. I could only laugh; the new house may be in a great location being only a block from the beach, but it definitely needed some work done, my mom called it T.L.C (Tender Loving Care). I felt it needed a lot more than that, like maybe a bulldozer.

I rushed through washing and conditioning my hair to conserve some of the limited hot water for shaving my legs. The sunny California weather was nice, and I definitely liked wearing shorts, but shaving my legs every day was getting old fast. At least it was better than wearing my regular attire of jeans and long johns like I would have to if we were still in Montana.

I was forced to switch off the shower when the hot water turned lukewarm. I toweled off with one of the plush rose colored towels my mom and I had special ordered when we still lived up north. We both hated stepping out of a hot shower and at least the plush towels helped ward off any chills. Of course, the mild temperatures in California were a lot different than the frigid temperatures we were used to.

I pulled on a pair of blue and green plaid board shorts and a Roxy t-shirt. I let out a sigh of contentment; I loved being able to wear such light weight clothes in March. Though before the move, I wouldn't have been able to tell you the difference between a Roxy shirt and the standard Target t-shirts I usually wore during the summers back in Montana. I have never been a name brand junkie, but there was no denying that the Roxy shirts were super comfortable, not to mention they were very flattering, even for someone as flat chested as me.

Of course starting tomorrow, I would be wearing a uniform everyday and my new Roxy shirts would have to wait until the weekends. This thought didn't make me cringe like most teenagers would have. I liked the idea of not having to decide what to wear each morning and never having to second guess my outfit choice. Even in the small town I had moved from, I had always been one step behind all the fashionistas.

I spent the hours waiting for my mom to wake up by getting my school supplies ready for the next day. I'd been out of school for two weeks for the move and had enjoyed my time off. I almost wished I had opted for early graduation. School had always been easy for me, but this past year it was ridiculously easy since I had finished all my core classes the year before. I had enough credits to graduate early, but I decided to do the whole graduation thing for my mom's sake. Being an only child, I didn't want to deprive her of my last few high school memories.

I was a little apprehensive about starting a new school, and hoped that I could remain unnoticed until I graduated. I just wanted to finish high school and move on to a big university where it would be easier to blend in.

I had organized my backpack about a million times and had stuffed it with plenty of notebooks, pens and pencils. I had also packed an extra book on the off chance that I forgot my current novel I was reading.

Finally, I set my backpack aside realizing it was as ready as it could be. I moved to my desk, but I was a perpetually neat person, so there really wasn't much to organize there. After a few minutes of just reshuffling things around, I sat on my bed.

Settling against my mountain of throw pillows, I picked up my favorite teddy bear that I had made at Build-a-Bear Workshop when I was ten. We bought it when we went to Las Vegas on vacation. It had become a ritual for my dad to buy me a new stuffed animal from B.A.B.W. every time we went on vacation, and I had a whole shelf of different animals we had purchased over the years. My favorites held court on my bed; like the cute orange tabby cat that we had bought in Orlando and the monkey from our trip to Colorado. Each one was special to me since my dad had helped me pick all of them out. I had fourteen in all, to remember every trip we had taken together.

I held my bear loosely in my hands as I studied the ceiling trying to keep my mind off the topic that was lurking in the back of my mind. At first I was successful as I studied the fine cracks that boarded the crease where the wall met the ceiling. The cracks had alarmed me at first, but mom explained that they were common in houses that were built on softer soil.

"We can hire somebody to caulk over them and then repaint the walls," she had said.

After a few minutes, I could no longer ward off the thoughts from the twist my dreams had taken. I had a nagging feeling that something was going to happen.

From the moment we entered Santa Cruz, I knew this was where I was supposed to be. If asked why, I would not be able to give you a straight answer, it was just a feeling I carried around in my heart.

I had done plenty of research on the city over the years and knew probably more about it than the locals. I knew before we moved here that there were approximately 58,000 people who lived within the city limits and that the city itself was 12 square miles. I knew that it was 74 miles south of San Francisco and 30 miles away from San Jose. I even knew that Santa Cruz meant "Holy Cross." I knew all of these things, but

I didn't know the most important thing, which was why I felt I had to be here.

I planned on finding out some of the answers today. My mom and I were going to visit the Boardwalk that had made Santa Cruz popular. When I found out that Santa Cruz had an amusement park on the beach, I wasn't surprised, it all seemed to fit. In the background of every one of my dreams, I could make out an amusement park in the distance. I had researched the Boardwalk enough that I was pretty confident it would be the one from my dreams. If I was right, at least I would be moving in the right direction.

"Krista, are you ready? I want to get there before it gets too busy," my mom called up the stairs.

I patted Feline on the head and grabbed my purse before I headed downstairs.

My mom was waiting at the bottom of the stairs wearing a cute peach spaghetti strap sundress, with a light ivory quarter sleeve sweater over it. I couldn't help admiring her sense of style. She could pick something off the rack that looked ordinary and turn it into something extraordinary by just adding the right accessories. No matter how hard I had tried to mimic her style, I was never able to achieve the same results.

I was fashionably defective.

All the gardening my mom had been doing recently had given her skin a nice honey glow that seemed even richer against the pretty peach of the sundress. With the golden highlights throughout her hair from the sun, she looked ten years younger. I couldn't help wishing my dad could see just how lovely she was in this laid back atmosphere. My parents had often talked about their plans for retirement and had always planned on living near the ocean.

I avoided looking directly at her as I stopped at the bottom of the stairs to put on the cable knit sweater that I had left draped over the banister.

"I'm ready. I've been up for hours," I said, still diverting my face from her eagle eyes. I had used a liberal amount of cover up to try to minimize the obvious dark marks under my eyes, but though they were lighter, they still remained.

Thankfully, my mom was in a hurry and didn't give me a second glance as I grabbed the keys off the hall table and headed out the door and down the porch stairs.

I used my own keys to lock the front door while my mom started the car; I twisted the knob once to make sure the door was locked, and then skipped down the three shallow porch steps, glancing back over my shoulder to take another look at the house.

I felt a warm glow just looking at it. The front porch was one of my favorite things about the house. It was at least ten feet wide and ran the whole length of the house. My mom had placed an oversized swing on the far side of the porch. On the other side we had added two Adirondack chairs that we painted a clear blue that reminded us of the ocean that was just a block away. My mom had also hung baskets of flowers along the rafters that ran along the ceiling of the porch. The overall effect was nice and inviting and seemed to beg you to spend a long lazy day relaxing your cares away. Even the rustic paint job added to the overall charm of the house.

I climbed into the front seat of my mom's Focus and slammed the door behind me. The car was only a few years old, but for some reason the doors had started sticking after the move. I was convinced that it missed the arctic temperatures it was used to.

"I think the car is protesting the move," I joked to my mom.

My mom steered the car toward the downtown area, driving along the pretty roads that made up the town. I loved looking at the foreign sight of all the lush lawns and pretty flowers that seemed to be in abundance at this time of year. Back home, you were lucky if you could even see the ground under all the dirty gray snow that covered everything.

I looked out the window as we drove along the coast, admiring the beautiful houses that sat directly on the beach. I would have loved to live right on the beach, but even with the insurance money from my dad, they were still way out of our price range.

Soon we turned off the beach road onto Delaware St. and then made a left onto Pacific Ave. We had driven through the downtown area a couple of times, but had not had a chance to browse the stores yet. My mom saw an advertisement for the local art store that she wanted to check out.

There were no parking spots in front of the art store, so we wound up parking a block away, in a parking garage.

We took our time as we strolled down Pacific Ave. looking at all the store fronts. We passed an old fashioned hardware store, and I smiled at the dated posters hanging in the dusty windows that looked like they had been there since the fifties.

Next door was another store called Chocolate Galore that stopped me right in my tracks as I paused to drool over the attractive displays in the front window. The small sign on the door taunted me when I discovered that they were closed on Sundays. With one more regretful look at the inviting delicacies in the window, my mom finally succeeded in dragging me away.

"So long candy store," I said with great sadness. "I will be back."

My mom burst out laughing. "We'll get you your chocolate fix later."

Linking her arm through mine, I couldn't help joining in on her laughter. She knew I was a lost cause. What could I say?

I pushed the door to the art store open for my mom and followed behind until I abruptly ran into the back of her.

"You have to walk through the door if you want to browse," I joked.

Looking around, I could see why she had stopped so suddenly. I had never seen a store with so much stuff. The space was relatively small, but looked even smaller with the overflowing shelves. Only four rows made up the interior of the shop, but they were stuffed to the gills. The first row held painting supplies. They offered paint in every imaginable color and every kind of brand. There was acrylic paint, wood paint,

17

water colors, and even paint you could use on the sidewalk. They sold spray paint and small jars of paint for fabrics. Then there were the countless racks of paintbrushes, from as cheap as 99 cents, all the way up into the hundreds, which I personally couldn't imagine anyone spending that much money on one paintbrush.

I made my way down the next row, which was comprised of every kind of paper and writing utensil you could think of. Walking down the row slowly, I picked out a gel pen in purple. I tried it out on the scribble pad mounted to the rack and liked the easy flow of the ink. *It would make a good pen for school*, I thought, and picked out three more in different colors.

I browsed the shelves for a few more minutes with my mom, but I quickly became bored. I didn't have one lick of artistic ability in my whole body and looking at artistic stuff only reminded me of my shortcomings.

"Mom, I'm going to go check out the bookstore across the street. I want to see if they got in that new book I've been waiting for." I said, handing her the four pens I had picked out.

"That's fine, honey. I'll be over there in a little while," she said giving a preoccupied half wave of her hand.

I couldn't help smiling to myself as I headed out the door. I had seen that look on her face many times and knew it would be a while until she joined me. I couldn't say anything though; I knew that I often had that same look when I browsed the shelves of a bookstore. My mom always joked that when I entered a bookstore, I crossed into the "Twilight Zone," but I couldn't help it. I always seemed to lose track of time while I browsed the shelves of books and minutes could easily turn into hours.

I crossed the street and entered the quaint bookstore. The store was lit by multiple lamps set out on small tables, periodically throughout the store. The walls were painted a rich dusky rose color, which should have been all wrong, but it wasn't, the soft light of the lamps glowed on the walls, giving the whole store a nice warm welcoming feel to it.

I took a deep appreciative sniff as I entered the store. There was nothing like the smell of books, both new and old. If someone ever bottled the smell, I would be all over it.

I browsed the used section for a few minutes, checking to see if anything jumped out at me by any of my favorite authors that I may have missed. I jumped about a mile when I felt something brush against my leg. Looking down startled, I was relieved to see that it was just a cat rubbing at my feet.

I squatted down to pet him, as he rubbed against my legs purring his approval over my attention.

"Aren't you the sweetest of kitties?"

"He's just spoiled," a voice said behind me. I turned and found myself facing an attractive older woman wearing a t-shirt with the store logo on it.

"He seems happy here," I replied, blushing slightly. Talking to new people was always tough on me and even with my secret rule of no physical contact; I always seemed to get an intuitive insight to their current emotions.

"Oh, he is. Most customers don't mind him around so he gets lots of free attention. Was there anything I can help you find?"

"I'm looking for the Johanna Knox novel. Have you gotten it in yet?" I asked, blushing less this time. I was relieved that the clerk was so friendly and seemed to give out a positive vibe.

"They just came in. I haven't emptied the box yet, but if you give me a few minutes, I'll pull one out for you."

"That's great." I said, marveling at my luck. "I love your store; you have a nice selection of books. It's great to find a store that combines used and new books."

"So do I, which is why I originally opened this store. I wanted to give this area a nice place to relax and enjoy their favorite books."

"Well, I'm glad you did, it's hard to find a good bookstore that gives you the freedom to browse," I said with a smile.

"I'm glad you like it. I'll go unpack those books for you. Look around and then checkout the reading area I set up in the back of the store," she told me as she headed toward a small stack of boxes.

I was happy about my good fortune, and could already tell I would be spending many hours here in the future. I continued to look around, periodically pulling books off the shelves that caught my eye as I explored the store.

I couldn't help the happy sigh that escaped me when I saw the big overstuffed chairs set up for reading, and sighed again with contentment when I sat down.

My mom found me there an hour later with my nose stuck in the new book the clerk had kindly unpacked for me.

"Sorry I took so long, I couldn't decide what to buy," she said as she sat next to me in the other overstuffed chair. "Wow! These are great; remind me why we bought Lazy Boys and not these chairs?"

I raised my eyebrows at the many bags sitting at her feet. She just shrugged her shoulders.

"I know aren't they great?" I asked, deciding not to comment on the bags. She looked guilty enough, when she shouldn't be. "I love this store. The woman who owns it seems very nice and you should see her cat roaming around like he owns the place. Maybe I could try to get a summer job here," I said thoughtfully.

It would be fantastic to earn money working at a bookstore. I had been dreading the idea of finding a job, but I knew I needed to find something to do for summer break. At least if I worked at a bookstore, I might get a discount on the merchandise.

Before we left the store, I worked up the nerve to ask the owner for an application. The owner seemed pleased by my interest and told me to return it as soon as possible, that she would be hiring her summer help within the next month or so.

I felt lighthearted as we left the store. One less thing to worry about was definitely a plus in my book.

The drive to the Boardwalk was short and soon we were pulling into the parking lot. My mom grabbed some change out of the center console to feed the meter.

"Do you want to ride some rides?" she asked me as we walked across the smooth pavement.

"Not today, I thought it would be fun if we just walked around. Maybe even walk on the beach for awhile," I said trying to sound nonchalant as I subtly faced away from her. I didn't want my tell-all blush to giveaway the fact I was hiding something from her.

The view from the beach was the whole reason I wanted to visit the amusement park. Of course I couldn't tell her the real reason, so I had fabricated a story of wanting to see the famous amusement park by the sea as an excuse for the outing today.

Admission to the amusement park was free, so we were able to stroll right in. The park was busy with families trying to shove one last, fun day into their final day of spring break. I smiled as I watched kids run from one ride to next, followed behind by their parent's that already looked harassed even though the park had just opened. Older kids hung out in groups, trying to look cool without parental supervision. They seemed to like the roller coaster the most, since the line for that was the longest. It had a big sign above the entrance proclaiming it as the "Giant Dipper." A smaller sign informed riders that it was either 6 tickets or free with the purchase of an arm band.

We continued to stroll around, laughing at some of the rides, and the sanity of those that choose to ride them. One in particular caught our eye called *Double Shot* the whole purpose of it seemed to be to shoot people 125 feet in the air at a mind numbing speed.

22

"No thank you," my mom murmured as we passed it, looking slightly green in the face.

I laughed. My mom was definitely not a ride fanatic. That title had always been reserved for my dad. Just thinking about him made my heart ache. I couldn't help thinking how much he would have enjoyed the Boardwalk, and the atmosphere around it, with the cool rides and the smell of the ocean.

My mom stopped at one of the vendors to buy me my promised chocolate in the form of an ice cream. Just the smell of it made my mouth water. My mom laughed when she saw the look on my face. I returned the smile sheepishly. What could I say? Chocolate talked to my soul.

I finished my cone before I finally headed toward the stairs I had spotted earlier that lead down to the sand. I was filled with anticipation as we walked down the sandy concrete steps.

We paused at the bottom stair to remove our shoes.

I sighed in contentment as my feet touched the sand. I had been to beaches before, but never on the west coast. I knew I was crazy to think so, but to me the sand just felt better here. I loved how nice and cool it was as I dug my toes into it. Maybe I felt this way because I thought it might be our beach, the one from my dreams, but I couldn't help feeling like I belonged here.

My mom settled on the sand while I walked toward the ocean, pretending to look for shells. The breeze from the ocean pulled at the edge of my shirt as I approached the water. Shivering slightly in the cool sea breeze, I crossed my arms to hold my shirt in place and dipped my toes in the ice-cold water. The anticipation made me feel like I was going to burst, but I looked out at the endless sea for a few minutes as I worked up the nerve to turn around and see if it was the same amusement park from my dreams. I wasn't sure I could handle the disappointment if I was wrong.

Finally with no further apprehension, I slowly turned and felt my breath leave me in one big gasp.

I was standing on a spot that I had stood on hundreds of times. There was no denying that this was indeed the Boardwalk that I had seen so many times in my dreams. I looked around quickly, as if expecting to see him, and then shook my head at how ridiculous it would be if I did. Of course he was not here, he didn't even exist.

I must have seen a picture of the Boardwalk when I was younger and unconsciously added it into my dreams. I could find no other explanation that would justify why I had dreams about some place where I had never been.

I tried to contemplate what this could mean. Was I crazy or could this be real, and if it was real, did that mean he might actually exist somewhere? I didn't know what to think at this point. I had come here today hoping to get some answers; but ironically, I was more confused than ever.

Chapter 2

"Krista," my mom called up the stairs the next morning. "Are you ready for school?"

I glanced one last time in the mirror over my dresser, and cringed at the faint smudge lines under my eyes. *So much for cover up*, I thought ruefully. Last night had been another bad night. I decided to limit my make-up, knowing that to add blush to a face that turned red from embarrassment so easily would only make me resemble a clown in a circus. The only thing I added liberally was my foundation, which I hoped would cover up the smudges. I finished with a touch of eyeliner to bring out the color of my eyes, and finally my favorite cherry lip gloss from Bath and Body Works.

I had to admit that except for the dark marks, I actually looked halfway decent. The school uniform fit me nicely. The pleats in the skirt swished out with every step; the crisp white shirt was tucked pertly into my skirt, and the navy blue cardigan was knotted across my shoulders. My hair was thrown back in the customary ponytail I preferred to wear; since it aggravated me when my hair fell in my eyes while reading. To make the ponytail more appealing, I clipped a navy blue hair clip at its base.

"Well that's as good as it's going to get, Feline," I said, patting his head on my way out the door.

He sunk even deeper into my quilt, making me smile. At the end of the day, he would be there in the same spot. Sure, he would use the cat box and eat his food in the kitchen, but somehow he sensed when I would be arriving home, and he always waited for me in the same place.

I made my way down the staircase, pausing to take a deep breath and making sure I had a smile firmly on my face. My mom didn't need to worry, especially since we had just gotten our lives on a somewhat normal path. There was no need to ruin it.

"Hi mom," I said, kissing her on the cheek on the way to the refrigerator.

"Don't you look cute and sassy in your new school uniform?"

"Do you like?" I asked, twirling around, giving her the full effect of the pleated skirt.

"It looks very flattering on you honey, I'm so glad you finally get to go to a school where you feel comfortable."

"Me too, I just want to blend in with all the other smart kids in the school. Hopefully the teachers will be too busy with them to worry about me," I said grabbing the six-pack of chocolate cupcakes out of the refrigerator.

"Honey, I know you think you're going to blend in, but I hate to break it to you, you're special. Even these teachers are going to realize it."

"You're just biased. You have to think I'm special. You're my mom. It's written in the parent's handbook."

She raised her eyebrows as if to say, *are you kidding me?* She let it slide though, and instead focused on my face.

Crap. I hastily looked down and concentrated on taking the paper off my cupcake. My morning eating habits had been a battle for many years, but my parents and I had finally reached a truce when I had agreed to eat a healthy breakfast every other day. I won the arguments when I pointed out that cupcakes or chocolate brownies were the same as eating doughnuts or a sugary cereal for breakfast. Tomorrow I would have to choke down a whole grain bagel, but today I could enjoy my wonderful chocolate cupcake.

"He left again last night?" She asked.

I could tell by her worrisome tone that my ploy had not worked.

I mentally kicked myself for telling my mom about the new twist my dreams had taken. As long as the dreams made me happy, she was okay with me having them, but if they started making me sad, she'd bring up the topic of taking me to a sleep clinic to try to put a stop to them.

When my dad was alive, he had broached the subject of taking me to a clinic many times, but mom always intervened on my behalf. Of course if my mom knew how often I dreamed about him, she probably would have felt differently. As far as she knew, I only dreamt about him occasionally. My dad had serious issues when he found out that the boy in my dreams was aging with me. He was okay with it when I was young, but he didn't like the idea of me dreaming about some teenage boy.

"Mom, I'm fine," I said. "Don't worry about me."

"It's my job to worry about you. I don't like the idea of you getting so upset while you are sleeping," she glared at me. "And even though you try to cover it, I know that it's following you throughout your day. You're just getting over your dad; I hate to see you upset all over again."

"Mom, trust me, I'm fine. Come on, we need to get a move on or I'm going to be late for the first day of school."

By the look on her face, I knew the subject wasn't closed. Next time, I would have to do a better job at covering up the signs of my dreams.

We arrived at my new school with ten minutes to spare. "Are you sure you don't want me to go in with you?"

"No, I'll be fine. I have my schedule, and I've studied the school map enough that I shouldn't get lost." At least that's what I was hoping anyway.

"Try to make friends honey, okay?"

"Mom, you know I'm not good at that. People just don't like me."

"That's not true. People are just put off by the way you study them. Sometimes you look like your searching for something in them."

She was right of course; I was always sizing everyone up, searching for the same kind of connection with others that I shared with the unknown boy in my dreams.

"Look mom, I'll try, okay? It's just hard for me to meet new people."

"I know honey. I just want you to be happy."

"I'll try," I said again, getting out of the car.

I closed the car door behind me and looked at my new school. I couldn't help feeling a little awed at the beauty of the campus. The brochures didn't lie, it was a beautiful school. The building itself was two sprawling stories that was as big as the mall back home. The most appealing feature of the building was the wide staircase leading up to the large imposing front doors that were made from honey colored oak. Windows that sparkled in the bright sunlight lined the exterior of the building and were placed every six feet or so. Each window was adorned with a different brick inlay pattern over it. Ivy ran up the sides of the structure in abundance and made the school look more like an Ivy League college than a private high school.

It was definitely more prestigious looking than my previous high school. I couldn't help feeling intimidated just looking at it; I now knew why the tuition was so high. The grounds themselves probably cost more to maintain than my old school spent for all their teachers salaries put together. I had once gone golfing with my dad and even that grass couldn't compare to what surrounded this school. The grass was plentiful and was only broken up by the big oak trees that provided shade over the many picnic tables that littered the grounds. Beautiful flowers flanked the sidewalk leading up to the building, and ran along the border of the building. The overall effect was quite pretty, and I couldn't help being impressed.

Glancing at my wrist watch, I saw that I still had eight minutes until the bell rang. I looked around for a place to sit while I waited. All the picnic tables were occupied by students catching up on what they had done during spring break. By the sounds of it, most had enjoyed a *killer* party at some guy's house. Others had obviously spent their time partying at the beach during spring break, since many of the girls were showing off their new tan lines.

I mentally shook my head as I settled under one of the big oak trees. It didn't matter if they were smarter, teenagers are the same everywhere. I didn't know why I felt so out of touch with other kids my age. Maybe my mom was right, maybe I should try to make more of an effort to get to know people better. Maybe the connection I had been searching for all these years just didn't exist.

I studied a group of guys messing around with a Frisbee. They all looked so carefree and happy. Had I ever been that carefree? I couldn't remember a time when I wasn't thinking about *him* with some part of my brain. Could someone be carefree when they were always consumed with a hunger for something else?

A shadow fell across me. Looking up in surprise, I saw a very pretty girl looking down at me with interest.

30

"Aren't you afraid that you're going to get a grass stain on your skirt?"

"Excuse me?" I asked surprised. I wasn't used to someone talking to me; most times people treated me like a leaper.

"Aren't you afraid you're going to get a grass stain on your skirt?" the girl repeated.

"No, if I do, I'm sure it will wash."

The girl's face widened into a big smile. I felt my mouth spread into a matching smile.

"I knew you were my kind of girl when I saw you plop down without a care of your clothes. I'm not sure I've seen anyone sit on the grass since I started here six months ago." She said, still smiling

She held out her hand. "I'm Sam."

"I'm Krista," I said, reaching out to shake her hand. I gasped in surprise when I felt a small shock like one of those hand buzzers you might get from a joke store, except, Sam was holding nothing. It filled me with a warm feeling like I had been dunked in a steaming bathtub. It gave me a feeling of odd completeness.

"Did you feel that?" I asked in a shocked voice. "What was that?"

"That was strange," Sam replied, not looking quite as surprised as I felt. Instead she studied me with interest.

I felt a little flustered. It felt like déjà vu, or like we had met somewhere before, but that was impossible. The warmth from our handshake was still strong and I looked at my hand in amazement. Who was this girl?

31

Sam continued to study me with interest as I tried to make sense of what was going on.

Only mere seconds had passed, but I had the uncanny feeling that this girl and I were lifelong friends. I should feel foolish, but for some reason, I didn't.

Finally, Sam broke the silence. "My real name is Samantha, but I changed it to Sam. It fits me better, don't you think?"

It was like she opened a flood gate. Before I knew it, we were chatting away like we had known each other for years.

"Amazing, isn't it?" Sam asked after a few moments.

"I know, I can't believe it," I said, still a little flustered.

"They're so funny how all they do is talk about some party, or whether their tan line is even," Sam said, echoing my thoughts from earlier.

"Huh?" What a dope I was, here I was thinking she was talking about our ease with each other. She was so easygoing; she probably had no idea the inner turmoil I was going through as I tried to figure out why I was so comfortable around her. Here I was trying to make heads or tails out of why I had felt a surge of electricity shoot through me when we had shaken hands, and she couldn't care less. She was probably this friendly with everyone and considered herself *the welcoming committee*. I felt my flush begin to deepen and looked down at the grass, mortified.

"I feel like I have nothing in common with any of them," Sam said.

I looked up surprised. Sam was studying the group with the Frisbee much the same way I had just done a few minutes ago. I laughed in relief.

"I can relate. I always feel that way in school, more like an observer, than a participant..."

I was interrupted when I noticed that Sam and I had become the topic of conversation for a group of guys walking by.

"Who's that sitting next to *fridge*," I heard one of them ask.

"I don't know, some new chick I guess, why, do you think you can score with her?" his friend asked.

Neither seemed to care that Sam and I could hear them. They stood there eyeing me like I was a steak or something.

I could feel a familiar wave of embarrassment approaching and tried to fight it back, but quickly realized it was too late. I knew that I needed to get out of there before Sam saw me get sick. The last thing I wanted was to puke in front of my new friend like a freak.

I scrambled to my feet. "I've got to go."

Dusting the grass abruptly off the seat of my skirt, I spared one last glance at Sam before darting off. I felt a twinge of guilt by the hurt look on her face.

The first bell rang as I rushed frantically through the halls searching for a restroom. Students jostled me on every side as they rushed off to their classes. It took me a few minutes to realize I had no idea where the nearest bathroom was.

What an idiot, I had neglected to look for bathrooms when studying the school map. Stepping out of the flow of traffic, I leaned against the wall trying to get my bearings back. I was hoping to avoid an episode like this on my first day at my new school. The sweat was beading quickly on my forehead, and I felt a burning sensation rising up into my throat. I tried to calm down quickly before I made a spectacle of myself.

I clamped my eyes shut, knowing from past experience this would help speed the process along. It was best to let the waves run their course and hopefully I wouldn't throw up. As soon as I could move again, I would find a drinking fountain and sneak some Advil. I didn't know what the school's policy was about taking over the counter medication. At my old school, you had to have a doctor's note on file in the school clinic in order to take Advil. I opted out of bringing one in for the new school figuring I would only be here for a few months. I figured if I had an attack, I could sneak some. Of course, I neglected to put any in my backpack that I had checked and rechecked the day before. I was a dope.

The waves finally slowed their attack on me and I felt like I was regaining control.

My thoughts were interrupted when I felt a water bottle being pressed into my left hand, and two pills being pushed into my right.

"Close your hand around the pills, they don't like you to take medicine without a note," Sam murmured in my ear.

I palmed the pills while I took a shaky drink of water. As the water flowed down my throat, some of the sickness from the emotional wave began to leave me. After a second drink, I was ready to swallow the pills. I knew real relief was about an hour away, but felt I might be able to make it to a bathroom. Making it to homeroom on time no longer seemed feasible, but looking like I might puke was not the first impression I wanted to make in my new school, anyway.

Sam took the water bottle from me as she grabbed onto my elbow and began to steer me down the hallway. When the fogginess in my head finally began to clear, I opened my eyes, but could only make out the shapes of the people we passed. My eyesight would return to normal in a few moments once the Advil began its work on my damaged nerves.

I was more than a little confused that Sam had known how desperately I needed the water and Advil. It was if she knew exactly what I was going through, which was ridiculous.

"Can I help you girls?" asked a kind elderly voice.

My eyes were finally fully focused and I saw that Sam had led me to the school clinic.

"Yeah, this is her first day, and I think nerves are making her sick," Sam replied.

"Oh! You poor dear. Follow me. I know how tough it is in a new school. Come lay down on a cot in the back."

"Can I come with her?" Sam asked. "I thought I could walk her to class when she's feeling better."

"That sounds fine dear. Just let me know if you need anything," she said as she patted me on the back on her way out.

I sat on the edge of the cot in the room which resembled a daybed more than a cot. In my old school, the cots were made of canvas and metal and smelled like the outdoors, and not in a good way.

Glancing around the room, I could see more benefits of going to a private school. Instead of the industrial steel gray color walls that made up the clinic of my old school, the walls in this room were painted a warm honey yellow. The color had an instant soothing feeling that started to ease my frazzled nerves. The yellow walls were broken up by white chair rails that ran the length of the walls. Above the chair rails were a series of appealing paintings. Each painting had the same exotic looking tree. At first glance they all looked the same, but when you studied them more closely, you could pick out subtle differences to distinguish between each one.

Sam sat in the easy chair next to the daybed where I was perched.

No folding chairs for private school, I thought as I studied the rich hardwood planks that made up the floors throughout the room. I shook my head slightly, thinking that even the flooring in this school was a far cry from the cracked linoleum floors that covered every square foot of flooring in my old high school.

"I'm sorry I walked away from you," I finally blurted, feeling slightly embarrassed.

36

"That's okay. I could tell that those guys embarrassed you. I could see it affecting you, trust me, I can relate. My nerves sometimes become frazzled in embarrassing situations, too."

"Um yeah, but mine seem to be worse than most people," I said understated. I knew for a fact that no one had emotions like mine.

"Well, you might be surprised," Sam said.

I shrugged it off not wanting to alienate myself with my new friend. There was no reason to show what a freak I was.

"Believe me; I've felt that way many times over the years." Sam said so empathetically, that for a brief moment I had the crazy notion that maybe she did know what I was going through.

I shook my head at my stupidity. I had once tried to look it up on the Internet, and many diseases showed similar symptoms to mine, but none of them were a perfect match. The doctors my parents took me to ran countless tests, but everything turned out inconclusive. They had planned on taking me to the Mayo clinic, but I pleaded with them to just give it a rest. I was sick of being poked and probed. After that, my parents tried to make light of my sensitivity issues and told me I was one of a kind. I had come to terms with the fact that I would always be a freak, and as long as I didn't humiliate myself by throwing-up in front of others I could live with it.

I thought about confiding in her just how out of control my emotions could get, but figured I would wait before I showed my true *freakish emotions* around her.

Sensing my mixed feelings, Sam changed the subject.

37

"So have you lived in Santa Cruz your whole life?" She asked.

"Um, no. We moved here a few weeks ago. I like it a lot and the weather is unreal."

"Yeah it's definitely easy to get used to. I've been here for awhile and have become quite spoiled wearing shorts most of the year. Of course I don't get much of chance to wear them here at this *prep party*," she said with a slight edge.

"You don't like it here?"

"Well, it's definitely not my ideal school choice, but my foster mom went here, and she was so excited when I got in, I didn't want to bust her bubble."

"Foster mom?' I asked, not wanting to intrude.

"Yeah, it's no big deal. I've been in foster care pretty much my whole life. This new set is pretty cool though, and it looks like they're going to keep me until I'm legal, which is sweet because it's a drag to constantly pack up your crap to move to a new location."

I could tell it wasn't quite as blasé as she was making it, but I didn't push the subject.

Briiiiing.

I jumped as the bell above my cot rang.

I glanced at my watch, shocked; we had spent all of our homeroom period talking. I was never one to skip class, so I was surprised that I didn't feel guilty about skipping. Maybe it was the fact that this seemed to be so much more important than some class. After all, I had just met a girl who I could finally relate to. The mere idea of it was too cool.

We scrambled to our feet, grabbing our book bags off the wood floors. With wide smiles on our faces, we both raced out the door together.

Even though the clinic was hopping with students trying to get out of class, the school nurse noticed our hasty departure and yelled after us.

"You girls better hurry."

"We will," Sam yelled back over her shoulder.

"What's your first class?" Sam asked, trying to catch her breath after we finally slowed down.

"Let me see," I said, pulling my schedule out of the front pocket of my book bag. I handed it over to her.

"Oh good, we share all the same classes, except fourth period. That works out great; fourth period is just before lunch. We can meet back up and eat lunch together."

I was relieved to hear that Sam shared most of my classes. Though I was a little disappointed our schedules didn't match up completely, but beggars can't be choosers.

I glanced at my schedule and was relieved that I at least had Reading for fourth period. Reading was of course my best subject, and at least I could bury my nose in a book during class. Most reading teachers expected the same thing, read a story and either write a report on it, or answer a series of questions.

Sam glanced over and looked at my schedule.

"At least you have Mrs. Rod for reading. She's a piece of cake as long as you bring your own book. She assigns an essay every six weeks on the book your reading, grades it, then averages the grades together, and that's your grade for the class," she said confirming my thoughts. "That's if you like to read."

"I love to read," I replied once again, surprised that here was something else we had in common. I could tell by the look on Sam's face that she was surprised also.

We made it to first period just as the bell rang. Sam slid in her seat in the back of the room, while I waited up at the front for the teacher.

As the room filled up, I could feel the many stares of the other students in the class. I felt my face start to flush as I studied the ground. I hated being the center of attention and would have welcomed it if the ground opened up and swallowed me whole. Then I remembered Sam was in the class, I looked up and met the many stares head on. I scanned the faces; finally settling on Sam's and felt my panic begin to subside as I realized that for the first time ever that I was not alone in school.

As if she could read my mind, Sam smiled at me and made a crooked face at the back of all the students watching me.

I almost laughed out loud, but managed to stifle it before it could erupt out of me. I couldn't contain the wide smile that spread across my face.

I noticed that a few of the boys in the class sat up straighter and looked at me appreciatively like my smile was for them. More than a few of them leered at me in a more vulgar way.

I choked back a half-laugh at their looks; I wouldn't give them the time of day. I was only interested in one guy, and though I knew it was juvenile to carry a torch for some dream guy, I couldn't help myself.

I was assigned to a seat that was in the back and two rows away from Sam's. I was relieved that it was in the back of the room. My moment of bravery had faded and I was more than ready for everyone to stop staring at me.

First period dragged. I had taken all the math classes required at my previous school, but St. Briggets expected me to take four years of math to graduate. The math was easy and I could have done the problems in my sleep. I finished the twenty problems with half the period still remaining. I glanced at Sam; she had her nose already buried in a book she had pulled out of her bag.

Usually, I would pretend to continue working so that I would not attract attention to myself, but as I watched Sam reading, I decided to follow suit. I was going to try to turn over a new leaf and stop trying to fade into the background so much.

With Sam's help, I made it through the next two classes, and by fourth period I was ready to tackle it alone. Sam's positive attitude was beginning to rub off on me and I felt surprisingly confident. We had sat next to each other in the last two classes and passed the time by sneaking notes back and forth.

We split up outside Mrs. Rod's class.

"I'll meet you in front of the cafeteria," Sam said as she hurried off to her own class.

Mrs. Rod was at her desk when I entered the room. She handed me back my schedule and explained the simple class rules, and then told me to choose a seat anywhere.

In typical fashion, I chose a seat in the back of the room and pulled out my current book. Thumbing it open to the page I left off on, I started to read until I realized I really wasn't paying attention to it.

My mind was preoccupied by the things Sam and I seemed to share. It was just a little wacky that we had so much in common. Like the fact that she had been in foster care, and I was adopted. It seemed odd that both of us were being raised by people other than our real parents. That, combined with the fact that Sam claimed to have *emotional issues* also... Were adopted kids just more sensitive, and did I just have a stronger case of it?

"He's a babe," a short mousy looking girl all but squealed to her seat mate. "Have you seen him?" she asked.

My thoughts were interrupted by a conversation going on in front of me.

"Yeah, I saw him. He's totally hot, he looks barely older than us, but he has to be older, otherwise he wouldn't be able to intern here. I bet he's no older than twenty though," replied her seatmate.

"I don't care how old he is," piped in a third voice, "I would love to spend some quality detention time with him."

I couldn't believe they were talking about an intern like that, he was practically their teacher. I thought it showed bad taste to be panting after some teacher. I was raised to respect my teachers and to treat them like you would treat a parent.

I shot a look of disgust at them and then re-opened my book. This time I was able to lose myself in the pages and before I knew it the bell was ringing.

I gathered up my things and headed out of the room ready to distance myself from the gossiping girls. They had talked through the whole period, and though I had been able to tune out their words, their annoying voices were harder to ignore.

Sam was waiting for me right where she said she would be.

"Do you buy or brown bag it?" she asked.

"Brown bag," I said, holding up my lunch for her to see.

"Good! Me too, let's eat outside, it's a nice day."

Everyone had the same idea and many of the seats were taken up outside. We headed for a big oak tree and settled under it.

"We could never do this at my old school."

"Where was your old school?" Sam asked.

"A pinpoint town on a map, called Bozeman."

"I've never heard of it."

"It's way up north in Monta...."

"Oh my God, he is so gorgeous..." squealed a nearby voice.

I barely controlled my groan. *Great.* The gossip hounds were back and they were obviously still talking about the new intern.

Sam laughed at the look on my face. "I see you've met our *Lush Trio*," she said in a low voice.

I let out a loud unexpected snort of laughter. My burst momentarily snagged the attention of the trio. They turned and glared at me for a moment, like I was unworthy to interrupt their conversation.

"*Lush Trio*, that's perfect," I told Sam in a quieter voice.

"It fits them to a tee. They are always discussing some guy or texting each other pictures of some guy that grabs their attention."

I looked over and sure enough, they were huddled around one of their phones, obviously looking at the picture of the *Hot Intern*. I was surprised they had their cell phones out. In my old school, cell phones had to stay in your book bag all day with the ringer off. If a teacher saw your phone out, or heard it ringing, they would confiscate it.

I commented on this to Sam. "Oh they tried to set the same rules here, but after a few angry calls from some of the parents, the Dean changed his mind. You're still supposed to have them off during class time, but nobody listens, they just turn the volume down."

"My mom would have a stroke if she caught me ogling a teacher or an *intern*," I said a little louder than intended.

My remark gained the attention of the trio once again.

Sam and I snorted at the trio's obvious disgust as they stalked away. I was definitely not winning any brownie points with them.

After the trio's departure, Sam and I talked about trivial things. Favorite books, movies, and other likes and dislikes. We were amazed at the many ways we were alike, and joked that we could be long lost twins, separated at birth.

"I'd buy it if we looked even remotely alike," Sam quipped.

She had a point. I was nearly 5' 8" almost 7" taller than her. Not to mention the fact that she was cute and petite and looked like she belonged on some football field, cheering her team on. Plus, she had movie star brown hair that swung from her shoulder like an advertisement for a shampoo commercial. Her skin glowed from a natural tan, which helped to accentuate her warm brown eyes. If she was taller, she would have made a great model. I felt extremely plain, just standing next to her.

The bell rang as we finished our lunch. Tossing our trash in a wooden trash barrel, we headed toward our fifth period class. We would finally meet the much talked about young male intern that had all the girls buzzing throughout the school.

Sam and I choose seats together. Sam pulled out her book while I took out a notebook.

This was my first world history class, and I was looking forward to it. I was a secret history buff and enjoyed learning about other countries. My mom and I often watched the History channel together at night.

I looked over at Sam to ask her a question, but she was already engrossed in her book. Deciding not to interrupt her, I pulled out a pen and started doodling in the margin of my paper.

I knew the instant the new intern walked in the door. Every girl except for Sam and I seemed to sigh. "Oh brother," I muttered without looking up.

Sam stifled a snigger as she continued to read, she had also heard the sigh of adoration from all the girls.

"All right, no books needed today. Instead, we're going to do a warm up exercise to get to know each other," said a warm masculine voice.

Chapter 3

I looked up in surprise; the voice seemed so familiar. I raised my eyes and found them locked on the warmest brown eyes I had ever seen. They were like pools of hot melted chocolate. I felt like I was swimming in them. Finally pulling my eyes away from his, I scanned the rest of his face. All the girls were right; he was the most handsome man I had ever seen. His lips were full and inviting with cheekbones just high enough for his perfectly chiseled face to give him a gentle ruggedness. I wondered if his golden honey colored skin was as soft and warm as it looked. His light auburn hair was just long enough to run my fingers through.

Wait a minute. This is a teacher, well, almost a teacher but still, to be sitting here daydreaming about touching his skin and running my fingers through his hair? What was wrong with me? I have never looked at another guy like this, and here I was fantasizing about my teacher. Except that, he didn't look like a typical teacher. He looked only slightly older than the students sitting in his class. I knew that was no excuse, but I was desperately trying to justify my strange reaction to him.

I looked down at my desk to regain my dignity, and then glanced over at Sam, who gave me a puzzled look. She seemed to sense that something was going on. I looked away so Sam could not read my face.

I heard the scratching of chalk and looked up as he wrote his name on the board. Mark Russo. *A regular name for a regular guy*, I thought. "Just a regular guy, regular guy, regular guy," I chanted to myself. If he's a regular guy, why is my heart racing like I ran a marathon? It was true; my heart felt like it was going to beat right out of my chest. My mom had encouraged me to give others a chance, but this was ridiculous and surely not what she had in mind.

"I'm going to write a few things about myself on the board and while I do that, I want you to answer the questions I've written down on the worksheet. This will help us get to know each other while I am here," he told the class.

I was still staring at his name on the board when he turned around. I meant to look down, but it was too late. The moment his eyes met mine, it was worse than the first time. I felt like someone had sucked all of the air out of me, and had to fight to catch my breath. The strange thing was that it seemed to affect him the same way. I could see that his knuckles had turned white where he gripped the desk. Fortunately, no one but Sam seemed to be aware that anything was going on.

He finally broke eye contact with me and began to pass out the papers. He passed them out individually instead of just handing a stack to each row to pass back.

My heart raced faster when I realized that in a moment he would be standing right beside me.

My palms began to sweat as he approached, and my breath came out in shallow gasps. I had no idea what was happening to me. I felt like a star struck celebrity watcher who was drunk off his presence.

Finally, after what seemed like an eternity, he was standing beside me. I willed myself not to look up, but I had no control. It was like some invisible force was governing my every action.

Our hands touched as he handed me the paper, and suddenly I was assaulted by a flood of unexplainable feelings of familiarity, almost as if we had already met before.

I felt myself fading away to where nothing else mattered except holding his hand and never letting go. The draw of his touch was magnetic. I didn't know who he was, but I no longer cared.

Someone snickered behind me. "Guess she's not the goody two-shoes she was trying to portray earlier," said a snide voice that I recognized as one of the trio's.

He stepped back, breaking our connection. I had to bite back a cry of distress as I felt his hand pull away. My hand suddenly felt incomplete away from his and I could see by the look on his face that he felt it also.

He walked down the rest of the aisles and made quick work of passing out the rest of the papers. I watched his retreating back, wondering what all of this could mean.

He wrote examples on the chalkboard of what kind of information we should include on the sheet that was handed out. He was currently a student at UC of Santa Cruz, and had gotten his masters degree the year before in physics, and was finishing up his PH.D. The next item he added was that he was interning at the school for his thesis, but it was the last bit of information that created a buzz among the students, his date of birth. It didn't take a math genius to figure out that he was only eighteen.

The rest of the class passed in a blur for me as I tried to come to terms with what it all meant.

I had never even looked at another guy, let alone fantasized like this. He was practically an adult for goodness sake, although he was, only a year older. Still, I wasn't the type of girl to chase after some guy, especially a teacher. I was ashamed with the way I was acting. There must be a simple explanation for my reaction to him.

The bell rang.

I looked at the empty paper in front of me and crumpled it into a ball.

Sam and I stood up together and filed toward the front of the room. Sam dropped her paper off on his desk while I threw my blank one away. We were the last two in the room, and as we passed him on our way out, I vowed to ignore him and kept my eyes firmly on the ground as I shuffled out of the room.

I felt a slight pressure in my hand as I passed by him. I looked and was surprised to see a folded up paper in the palm of my hand. He had passed me a note taking care to not to touch my skin. I looked at him one last time as I left the room, and was surprised at the expression on his face.

He seemed pleased, like he knew something I didn't.

Sam looked intrigued as we walked down the hall.

"What was that all about?" She asked.

"I don't know," I replied, slightly embarrassed. "I felt a connection like when you and I met, but a hundred times stronger. I was drawn to him like I have never been drawn to anyone else. Strange, isn't it?" I asked, not sure what Sam would think.

Sam looked thoughtful, like she was trying to figure something out. "Yeah, it is strange," she said at long last.

The rest of the day passed in a blur. I went through the motions, but my mind was lost, wrapped up in thoughts about *him*.

I had always thought the idea of love at first sight was silly, but there was definitely something irresistible about him, and not just because of his strikingly good looks. This was something kindred, my hand still tingled from his touch, and I had an odd warm sensation throughout my whole body.

This is crazy, I thought to myself. *It would never work.* First of all, my mom would freak if I came home and told her I wanted to date an intern teacher from my school, and second, the school would obviously not allow it.

"Krista, are you there? Hello, anyone in there?" Sam asked, snapping her fingers in front of my face.

51

I shook my head to clear away his image. The last bell for the day must have rung, because only Sam and I remained in the classroom. Even the teacher had left the room.

"What a wasted day of school that was," I muttered to Sam, as we gathered our books and headed out the door.

"Missed homeroom, neglected to do the assignment in fifth period, and then proceeded to sit through the rest of the day like a zombie. My mom would be real pleased if she heard how my day had gone," I said with disgust ringing in my voice.

"Hey give yourself a break, first days are always tough. Take it from me; I've had plenty of first days." Sam said, even though she seemed to sense there was more to it than first day jitters.

"Did you ever read that note he passed you?"

So, Sam had seen him pass me the note.

"No, I wasn't sure if I wanted to."

"Why not?"

"Because, you saw what happened in there, he's an intern. I don't know what came over me. I don't check out guys, and I don't act like he's the only person in the world in front of a bunch of people I've never met."

"Well, you may not, but it's hard to deny that something happened in there. We may have just met today, but I could tell you felt something in there. I think you should read the note, he obviously felt it too. He looked like he had been hit by a truck when he first saw you."

I thought about Sam's words, she was right. I should at least read his note. It had been burning a hole in my pocket the whole afternoon.

With shaking fingers, I pulled the note out of my pocket and stopped walking to read it. Sam stepped discreetly away, sensing that I needed a moment by myself to read it.

I smoothed out the creases of the note before I read it, dragging out the procedure while I mentally prepared myself. My heart skipped a beat at the words written on the paper.

We need to talk. I know you're confused, I can explain everything, meet me at the park after school.

Love always M.R

My heart started racing. What could he explain? What did he know that I didn't?

"Are you going meet him after school?" asked Sam, reading the note over my shoulder.

"I don't think so."

"Seriously? Why not?"

"Because I'm confused, I don't know what to make of all of this."

"Can I come over to your house?" Sam asked suddenly.

"Sure." I said surprised. "My mom won't be home until later, she wanted to drive to some art supply store she heard about. She left me pizza money; you can eat over if you want?"

"Sure," said Sam. "Your mom's an artist?"

"Well, no, but she's going to try her hand in it. She's taking a year off from work to dabble in it. My dad left us enough money for her to try new things."

"That sounds great," said Sam with just a tinge of envy in her voice. "It sounds like you two are close."

"They were there for me when I needed them the most. Once the judge had officially cut all the red tape after I was found, and allowed them to adopt me, they were ecstatic. They officially adopted me the day I turned six, and it was a great birthday present."

Sam's face took on a shocked expression.

"You were abandoned?"

I could have kicked myself, after years of keeping my abandonment a secret from everyone, I had let it slip out with someone I had just met. Of course, I felt a kinship with Sam, but I still couldn't believe I had let my guard down.

"I was found at a rest stop when I was two," I answered uncomfortably.

"I was put in foster care when I was two," Sam said in a voice laced with surprise.

"You were?" I asked, not quite believing her. Was Sam some kind of freak that made things up to make herself seem more interesting?

I felt myself freaking out. I couldn't help feeling like someone was playing some kind of joke on me, first with Mark and now Sam. I would have believed that this was their idea of a good way to torment me if Sam didn't look as surprised as I felt.

Sam must have felt the same, because she looked at me to see if I was pulling her leg. "You're kidding me, right?"

"No, I wish I was. All of this is wigging me out," I replied.

"Well to tell you the truth, I'm relieved. We can be freaks together," Sam said, trying to lighten the mood.

I smiled a half smile. It was hard not to respond to Sam's positive attitude. I had always been the glass half empty kind of person, but Sam was obviously a glass half full person.

We walked the rest of the way to my house in silence, both of us lost in the thoughts that were circling around in our heads.

By the time we reached my house, we both were sweating slightly from the short walk. I pulled open the fridge and grabbed two waters and two chocolate bars. My mom bought chocolate candy in bulk for me. I often joked that a candy bar a day, kept the doctor away. My mom had given up years ago, and as long as I brushed my teeth twice a day, she kept me stocked with chocolate.

I handed one of the bars to Sam, who was studying all the family pictures around our small house.

"My mom loves to take pictures," I explained. "She hates photo albums though, so most of our pictures wind up in a frame, or get thrown into a box."

"That's me right after they found me," I said, when I noticed Sam studying a picture of me where I was crying. My mom had told me that all I wanted to do was sleep. I never had to ask why, I already knew, he had been in my dreams, even then.

"I'm hungry," I said, changing the subject. "Let's order the pizza now, and listen to music upstairs while we wait for it."

After ordering the pizza, we headed upstairs to my domain, which was more like a loft than a full upstairs. It was narrower than the space below, and consisted of my room, a bathroom, and a small sitting room between the bathroom and my room. The only other door upstairs of course, led to the hall closet that I kept mistaking as the bathroom.

"This is pretty," Sam commented, as we settled into the chairs in the sitting area.

"Thanks. My mom and I wanted to make it a comfortable, soothing space."

We had worked hard to create just the right look. We painted the walls a nice warm taupe that glowed when the sunlight hit them and placed bookshelves from floor to ceiling around the room for the many books we had both read over the years. In between the bookshelves we placed framed posters of some of our favorite books. The frames were made from the same tasteful wood as the bookshelves. We searched high and low for the two comfortable lazy boys that sat in the middle of the room. Both of us could read for hours, so we wanted to be comfortable. The last touch was a sturdy table to sit between the two chairs. We liked to snack while we read, so having a durable table to hold our drinks was a must.

"I'll put some music on," I said. "Do you have any preference?"

"No. Anything is fine."

We listened to the music and talked until we heard the doorbell ring. After paying the delivery guy, I grabbed a couple sodas, and some paper plates and napkins.

We ate in silence, enjoying the cheesy pizza with its hearty sauce. Finally after dinner, Sam looked at me with a serious look on her face. "I've been putting off mentioning this, but I think we should make a list of things we have in common," she told me. "That way, we'll have a better idea of what we're dealing with."

I had to agree with her. I had been trying to ignore it all day, but it had become glaringly obvious that Sam and I shared some kind of link. I grabbed a notebook and started taking notes on our commonalities. Sam filled in the ones I had forgotten, making a point to mention our common defective "emotions," as she liked to put it, of course I still didn't believe that her emotional "madness" was the same as mine. Finally, I set the pencil down. "I think that's it."

"You forgot the biggest one," Sam said quietly.

"What's that?" I asked, looking up in surprise, I thought we had them all.

"You forgot to write down the dreams," Sam said in the same quiet voice.

"What dreams?" I asked, suddenly starting to feel panicked.

"The dreams we have about the guys?"

"How do you know about that?" I asked, standing up abruptly, suddenly very angry. The notebook slid off my lap and landed on the floor at my feet. I gave it no notice, as I felt the emotional wave approaching.

"I think you should leave," I told Sam, trying to fight down the nausea. I didn't know what kind of game Sam was playing, but I wanted no part of it. The anger began to engulf me; I knew I was on the verge of getting sick.

I rushed into my bathroom and threw-up immediately. It had been a long time since my emotions had made me sick enough to throw up. The retching finally ended as the waves receded. I rested my forehead weakly against the cool porcelain on the side of the tub.

I felt a cool cloth being placed on the nap of my sweaty neck. I wasn't surprised that Sam had stuck around. Though I tried to convince myself that she was playing some kind of game, I knew we had far too much in common to be just a coincidence. I didn't know what was going on, but I did know, it wasn't Sam's fault.

Sam handed me a glass of water. I looked up to see her studying me.

"I'll teach you how to fight the sickness back," she promised.

I just nodded my head weakly, not surprised that Sam somehow knew how to fight it off; she seemed so much stronger than me. She helped pull me into a standing position. My legs felt like cooked spaghetti, but I thought I could make it to one of the chairs. Sam took my arm and helped me settle into the chair.

"I know about your dreams because I have the same ones," Sam said, with tears in her eyes. "I didn't mean to make you sick."

"How did you know that I had the dreams?"

"I didn't know when I first met you. I suspected it after I saw your reaction in class today, but I knew for sure after I read the note."

"What do you mean?" I asked, more confused than ever. "What happened in class for you to suspect it, and why did the note convince you?"

"Because, I've been in your shoes before, I have the same dreams as you, and I felt the same way when I met the boy that had shared my dreams my entire life. Through all my crummy foster homes, he was always there for me, and when I met him it was like I had been hit by lighting."

"You've met your dream guy?" I asked surprised, not because she had dreams like mine (which was crazy), but because she made it seem like our dream guys were flesh and blood.

"You've met yours too. Surely you knew as soon as you saw him today, that he was the one?"

I shook my head in denial. "I've never seen his face though, how can you be so sure it's Mark?"

"Have you ever reacted like that with anyone else?" she asked, incredulous.

"Well no, but how do I know it's not just a normal reaction? He is attractive. You saw how all the other girls were ogling him," I said, trying to take just an ounce of crazy out of this situation.

Sam sighed, "Krista, come on, do you really believe that? If I'm right, that's what Mark meant in his note. He can explain. He already knows who you are. That's what I think, and he

59

knows it. Think about what he wrote in the note. He's your dream guy."

Dream guy. I rolled the words around in my head. I had always hoped the dreams meant something, that I would someday meet the guy of my dreams. Could all of this be real? I shook my head. I just couldn't believe it. We weren't some characters in some B-rated Sci-Fi movie.

"Are you feeling better?" Sam asked, interrupting my thoughts.

"Yes."

"I'm going to call my foster dad to come get me so you can rest," Sam said. "I really am sorry, I know how badly you're feeling. I just didn't know how to bring it up. I know it's freaky, but I am glad that I'm not alone."

"It all just seems so strange, that all of us would meet on the same day," I mused, almost to myself.

"It is strange, but to add more craziness to this whole mixture, when I woke this morning, I had the strangest feeling that something was going to happen today."

"What do you mean you felt something?"

"I don't know, I just felt an odd sense of anticipation I guess, like a premonition or something," Sam said as she dialed her foster dad's number. She rattled off the directions to my house for him and then hung up. "He'll be here in fifteen minutes," she said, perching on the on the edge of the other chair to wait.

While we waited, we discussed our common bond a little bit more, but didn't mention "dream guys" again. My emotions were a wreck and I needed time to allow them to recover.

Our conversation was interrupted by a knock on the door.

I was feeling a little better, so I walked Sam downstairs.

I opened the door to a distinguished looking gentleman. He was of medium height, but seemed taller by the well cut suit he was wearing. With just a few gray streaks through his hair, I would guess him to be about my mom's age.

"Hi. I'm Tom Harrison. You must be Krista. My wife Karen and I were thrilled when Sam asked if she could come over to your house today. We've been concerned that Sam hasn't made any friends since she moved in with us."

I heard Sam groan, obviously wishing he wouldn't have added that last part, the pained look on her face made that clear. I smiled; I could relate.

"I'll see you tomorrow, okay," Sam said, giving me a quick hug.

I locked the front doors behind them and headed up to take a quick shower before bed. I paused by a table at the foot of the stairs to scrawl a quick note to my mom.

Mom had a great day at school. I'll tell you about it tomorrow morning. Love Ya.

I knew I was taking the chicken's way out, but I wasn't ready to face my mom. I had already decided that I was going to keep her in the dark as much as I could. I was sick of being the constant source of worry for her. It was time for her to have the freedom to focus her energy on things that mattered to her, instead of always having to worry about my problems.

It dawned on me as I headed upstairs that I didn't even ask Sam about the guy that was supposedly her *dream guy*. I hope he wasn't some freak that had preyed on some young girl who might have confided in her dreams, too. I felt a sick feeling in the pit of my stomach. What if Sam's theory was wrong? I felt a wave of grief approach at the thought that Mark was just a regular person. I didn't want to admit it to Sam, but a small kernel of hope had awakened in my heart that Mark might somehow be the person I had been dreaming about for years.

With a million thoughts swirling through my head, I twisted the shower nozzle all the way to hot. The hot water helped to ease away the chills that always followed an attack. Once my shower was over, I blow dried my hair and put on warm comfy pajamas before I headed to my room.

I took a few moments to give Feline the attention he craved. After petting him for a few minutes, he settled down on the bed beside me. I reached over and flipped off the lights. The emotional upheaval of the day had left me exhausted and I fell into a quick slumber.

I knew I was dreaming. It was the same as always. I walked to the edge of the tide line where we always met. He was already there waiting in the shadows, but as I approached; he stepped out of the shadows for the first time. My breath escaped me. How had I missed it? Of course I knew him. Hadn't he visited me every night? Wasn't it his hand that I had held thousands of times in my dreams? Even though I had been expecting it, I was unprepared for the emotions that assaulted me when our eyes met. All I could think was, *IT'S HIM.*

Chapter 4

I woke to my own sobbing. I stuffed a hand over my mouth so my mom wouldn't hear. I didn't know how much longer I could take this heartbreak. The dreams, that for so long were my only source of comfort had now become nightmares.

I sat up pulling my knees tightly against my chest, rocking back and forth. My swollen eyes were sensitive to the touch as I wiped away the warm tears.

Feline jumped up beside me on the bed. He could always tell when I needed comfort. His soft fur and the mild vibrations of his purring were soothing.

I glanced at the clock, 4:00 a.m. He had left me earlier than normal. I sat on my bed contemplating how well things had gone, especially since his face was no longer hidden by shadows. We still were unable to talk in the dream but it didn't matter, somehow we could sense what the other was feeling. The reflection from the moon had danced on the waves, and I had felt his heartbeat against my back as he gently stroked the side of my face. Then suddenly, he was abruptly jerked away, leaving me feeling like my own limbs had been taken with him.

My throat was as dry as the desert from the sobs that had torn through me. I walked as quietly as I could to the bathroom for some water, deciding when I got there that a nice warm shower would be the best way to wash away the chilling side effects of the dream.

I stayed in the shower for a long time, letting the warm water gently massage my aching body. When the warm water started to run out, I twisted the nozzle to turn it off and stepped out of the shower. After drying off, I headed to my room to throw on a sweatshirt and jeans. I still had almost three hours until I needed to get ready for school. The sun was just barely beginning to rise over the horizon.

I walked over to my window so I could watch it rise. I pulled the cord that hung down from my ancient blinds. The blinds made a loud rustling noise as they rolled up. We had discussed replacing the blinds with some cute curtains, but we kept putting it off. I was sick of the ugly blinds, so maybe I would replace them this weekend.

I caught a movement out of the corner of my eye. Someone was on our front lawn, but strangely enough, I felt no panic at all. For some reason I expected him to be there.

I stared at him for a few seconds trying to organize my thoughts and then I headed out the door and down the stairs. I had put off the talk yesterday, but I was ready for it now.

Opening the front door quietly, I stepped outside. I could feel him the moment I stepped over the threshold. The impact of looking at him was no different than it had been the day before. If anything, the pull seemed even stronger today.

"It's you?" I said.

"Yeah, it's me," he answered.

"You knew yesterday in class?"

"Yes, I knew the moment you looked up at me. It was like being punched in the stomach."

"Have you always been able to see my face?" I asked.

"For as long as I can remember," He replied.

"I've never been able to see your face.... until last night."

"I figured that out in class yesterday, when you looked so confused. I tried to tell you. I waited for you yesterday," he gently chided me.

"I know. I just needed time. I was so confused yesterday. There I was hitting on my teacher's intern in a class filled with other people," I said, still feeling slightly embarrassed.

"Why have you been leaving me?" I asked abruptly. I had meant to ask the question later, but I felt the answer to this question was the most important.

Mark looked confused. "I don't leave, you're the one who leaves......" he paused, as understanding dawned on both of us. Neither one of us wanted to leave in the dreams. Something else was pulling us apart.

"What does this mean?" I asked.

"I don't know. When did you move here?"

"A few weeks ago. OH!" I shrilled, suddenly aware. Why hadn't I seen it before? The dreams changed the first night in my new house, my first night in Santa Cruz.

66

"Why did my moving to California change our dreams?"

"I don't know."

He settled into the swing on the porch, placing his hands on his jean clad knees. I sat beside him as we silently pondered our dreams. It all seemed surreal to be sitting here next to him, when I had fantasized about this my whole life.

I sat with my hands folded in my lap, consciously aware that his hand was just inches away. I yearned to reach over and grab onto it, but I fought back the urge. Part of me was scared that his touch wouldn't be the same as yesterday, while the other part was afraid it would feel just as magical, and I wouldn't want to let go. Just when I knew I was fighting a losing battle, Mark took the matter out of my hands.

Mark reached over and took my hand firmly in his. Though I was expecting it, I still momentarily lost my breath. His touch made everything feel right. Our dreams no longer mattered. All I cared about was that we were together now. I had imagined this moment forever. Even though I thought I would never really meet him, somewhere in my heart of hearts, I had always hoped for it.

I knew it was crazy. People didn't go around meeting guys they had dreams about. This was real life not some science fiction novel. Dream Guys like this, just didn't exist. It went against everything I believed in, but looking down at our hands it was hard to deny the connection. Even with our hands lightly clasped together, I could feel the most pleasant warmth from his touch spread throughout my whole body.

He asked me what I was thinking. I tried to put it into words. I explained the confusion, and how all this just seemed unreal.

"I know. Yesterday when I first saw you, I felt the same way. I was so shocked. Here was a girl, I had only dreamed about, sitting just mere feet from me. At first I was going to ignore you, but that was before our hands met. That's when I knew for sure that I wasn't hallucinating. Your touch was so familiar, and at the same time so new. Here I was, acting like some junior high guy who had just met some hot model; instead of the professional I was supposed to be. I tried to ignore you through the rest of class, but by the end, I knew it was too late."

He brought up an important point that I had almost forgotten.

"How did you wind up at my high school?"

"School has always been easy for me. I skipped most of elementary school and graduated at the top of my class when I was fifteen. I received my bachelor's degree in two and half years. I had to work my tail off to convince the board of trustees to let me use St. Briggets for my thesis."

Okay, so now I knew how we had both wound up at St. Briggets, but it didn't make it any less bizarre. The fact that he was still an intern concerned me though.

"Have you always lived in Santa Cruz?"

"No, I lived in Arizona when I was younger.

"How long have you been here in Santa Cruz?"

"About five years. My dad and I moved here after my mom died."

"Why Santa Cruz?" I asked, sensing what his answer would be.

"I was drawn here."

I wasn't surprised. It made crazy sense that he would be drawn here also. I had been drawn here, Sam was here, and now he was too. What did this all mean? What was going on? I leaned forward and placed my head in my hands.

"What's the matter?"

"I met a girl yesterday at school. She was in your class yesterday with me, her name is Sam. Do you remember her?"

He laughed. "I didn't notice anyone yesterday, except you."

"Why, what does she have to do with us?"

Us. The way he said that gave me goose bumps. I liked it that he thought of us as a pair.

"She and I have a lot of things in common, too many to be a coincidence."

"What do you mean? What kinds of things?"

I suddenly felt uncomfortable. I wasn't sure if I was ready to tell him about all my downfalls. Would it ruin his illusions of me if he knew about all my quirks? I had always been such a private person, and in the course of twenty-four hours, I had already spilled my guts out to one person.

He seemed to sense my inner turmoil. "You can trust me," He said in a quiet voice.

"I know," I said. "I just don't want to change your opinion of me."

"There's nothing you could say that would ever change the way I feel about you."

I took a deep breath and told him everything. I first filled him in on my childhood, and how my adoptive parents had figured out my sensitivity to emotions. I told him how I had always been a loner. How I found comfort with him in my dreams when my dad died. I told him how I had always hoped that he was really out there, and not just some person that would only visit me in my dreams. I told him about the pull this city had on me. Then I told him about Sam, and how she seemed to be the carbon copy of me. How we felt a connection to each other that was similar to ours, but not as strong. I let all the words pour out of me while he sat there quietly holding my hand.

I looked down at the uneven boards and watched as a fat bug struggled over the cracks between the boards. Every so often, half of its body would fall between the groves and it would flounder around trying to work its way back out.

"Sam even suspected that you were the guy from my dreams," I continued on a little self-consciously.

"How did she know that?"

"Because, she has dreams just like ours."

"What do you mean she has dreams like us?" Mark asked amazed.

I told him everything we had discussed the night before. About having the same kind of dream, and that Sam had already met her dream guy.

I could tell that he was having a hard time believing me, just like I had with Sam.

"It had never occurred to me that there were other people out there just like us," he said, trying to grasp what he had just heard.

"Oh, I forgot to tell you something else bizarre." He raised his eyebrows at my choice of words.

I laughed. He was right of course; all of this was turbo-bizarre.

I filled him in on the circumstances surrounding both of us being left when we were young.

A few minutes passed in silence.

I looked up at him to see what he was thinking. I was concerned when I saw the troubled look on his face. Had I finally sprung too much information on him? I myself had a hard time dealing with all of it. It was a lot for someone to digest.

"Well I wasn't abandoned, but my mom's been dead since I was three," he finally said in an odd voice.

"Are you sensitive to emotions too?" I asked, probing further.

"No, but I'm strong."

"You mean from lifting weights, strong?"

"No, I've never had to lift weights. I'm not Hulk strong, more like; I just have the feeling that I could protect myself in a fight with anyone, and come out the victor. Plus, I was the only one in karate class who could break the wooden board the first time I tried," he said with a chuckle.

"Strong, hum, I like the sound of that," I murmured.

"You do, do you?" He said with amusement as he stood up. He took his hand and touched the side of my face. His touch sent shock waves through me; it felt like every bone in my body had liquefied.

"I know this is all overwhelming, but I am so glad you're here," he said simply.

"So am I."

"I better head home. I need to get ready for class," he said pulling away.

I frowned. I had forgotten for a brief moment that he worked at my school. What were we going to do about that?

Mark saw my frown. "What's the matter?" He asked.

"You're practically my teacher. I'm sure the Dean frowns on teachers dating students," I stated.

Mark smiled in relief. "Krista, I'm only on a two month stint here. I don't think they can tell me who I can and can't date. I mean, we shouldn't flaunt it or anything, but I don't think it's that big of a deal. If it makes you more comfortable we can keep it secret, so other students don't find out."

That could work. I wasn't crazy about the idea of the other students finding out, but if we kept it secret it could work. We could make it through the next couple of months keeping our relationship quiet. Lying to my mom would be a different story, but I wasn't ready to lay all of this on her now. We had always had a no lie policy and I knew from a young age, as long as I told the truth, punishments would be minimal. I would have to categorize this as more of a need to know basis.

"I think your mom's up," he said. "I better go if we are going to try to keep this secret." He ran his hand down the side of my face one last time, and with one more backwards look, he turned and walked off. He was halfway down the street, when my mom opened the front door.

"Honey, were you talking to that boy?" she asked, looking at Mark's retreating back.

"Yeah, he goes to my school. I saw him from my bedroom window and I came down to see what he was up to."

"Krista, you know it's dangerous to come outside and talk to strangers. You should have come and got me."

"He's okay mom, I met him in school yesterday."

"What did he want?"

"Nothing," I mumbled heading upstairs. "I need to get ready for school."

I felt a wave of guilt starting to consume me. I hurried up the stairs trying to control the strong emotion. *Need to know, need to know, need to know*, I chanted to myself as I reached my room. Sitting on my bed, I waited for the guilt to begin to leave my body. Chanting had helped, as long as I was protecting someone, it was easier to curb my emotions.

I lay back on my bed as the last waves left me. Feline jumped up on the bed next to me, hoping I would scratch him between his ears. "I met my dream guy," I told him, knowing my secret was safe with him. "He's as perfect as I always imagined he would be." Feline purred loudly as if he understood what I was telling him.

Chapter 5

Sam was waiting for me in front of the school like we had planned the night before. I got out of the car and waved her over. I might have to keep Mark a secret, but I could throw my mom a bone and introduce her to my first real friend.

"Sam, this is my mom, Cindy Miller," I said as I introduced them.

"Hi. Mrs. Miller, it's a pleasure to meet you," Sam said in an enthusiastic voice.

I could tell right away that my mom was taken in by Sam. It was hard not to respond to her enthusiasm.

"We better go mom. We'll see you after school." We had made plans the previous night to get together again after school.

"All right, it was nice to meet you, Sam." Bye honey, I'll see you guys after school." With one last wave she drove off.

"Your mom's very nice," Sam commented, as we headed toward the tree where we sat yesterday morning.

"Thanks, I think so too."

"So, I'm dying to know....was I right?"

75

It didn't take a rocket scientist to figure out what she was talking about. "Yeah, it was him, and the dream was fantastic all the way up until the end."

"He thinks there's more to our connections..."

"Whoa backup, when did you talk to him? Can you talk to each other in your dreams now?" confusion colored Sam's voice.

"I didn't have a chance to tell you. I talked to him this morning. He came over after we woke up from the dream."

"Oh my gosh, you have to tell me everything. Was he everything you expected? Is the connection between you still strong? What did you talk about?"

I laughed. "Slow down, I'll tell you everything."

"Ouch!"

I was interrupted by a sharp stinging pain on the side of my head. Something had struck me hard on my right temple. Looking down, I saw a softball lying on the grass beside me.

"Sorry about that," a guy said, jogging up to me.

He didn't look sorry though; on the contrary, he looked quite pleased with himself.

"Do you want me to kiss it and make it better?" He said in a suggestive voice.

"Oh, brother!" Sam said with disgust.

"What's it to you *fridge*? He said with contempt as he turned to look at Sam.

"So, what do you think, will a kiss make it better?" he asked, trying to lay on the charm.

"No thanks," I said with disgust, and turned my back on him.

"Hey, what's your problem? I was just trying to be friendly."

"I have enough friends," I said dismissively, waiting for him to leave.

Instead he looked at me with a nasty look on his face. "Oh I get it. You're not into guys," he said, looking suggestively between Sam and me.

"Go bother....." my words caught in my throat as another person joined our group. I looked up to see Mark standing beside me, and he was not happy.

He had caught the end of the exchange, and I could feel the anger vibrating off of him.

"Maybe a trip to the Dean's office will clean up your language," he said.

"Is that a threat?" the boy asked in a mocking voice. "Maybe the Dean would like to hear how you've taken an interest in our new student. Everyone's talking about how the two of you were ogling each other in class. No, I don't think you'll be talking to the Dean anytime soon," he said in the same mocking voice as he turned and sauntered off.

Mark started to go after him. "Don't," I said in a low voice, putting my hand on his arm.

My touch stopped him in his tracks. The connection was as strong as ever. "Everyone's watching, you have to walk away and act like nothing happened," I said in a low voice. "Otherwise our secret will be out sooner than we wanted."

Mark looked at me one last time, glancing at the spot where the softball had struck my head.

"It's fine. I'll go to the nurse's station and get some ice," I said. "Besides, the nurse and I are already friends."

Mark reached up his hand, as if to touch the sore spot.

I took a step back. "No you can't, I said glancing around. "Everyone's still watching." Please go to class, I'll meet you later," I pleaded, suddenly choking back tears. The pain in his eyes was almost too much to bear.

Finally, he walked away and I let out a bent up breath. "So much for keeping it a secret," I said to Sam in a shaky voice.

Sam had remained silent during the whole confrontation, but I could tell she was going to burst if I didn't fill her in on all the details.

"Come on, I'll explain on the way to the clinic," I said, grabbing onto her elbow, for once my emotions behaved.

By the time we reached the clinic, I had given Sam a basic idea of what Mark and I had discussed earlier that morning.

"You again," said the same elderly nurse from the day before. "What can I do for you today?"

"I got hit in the head by a softball and I think it may have cut my head a little. I was wondering if I could get some ice."

"Come around the counter and let me check it over."

I walked around the counter and sat on the padded stool the nurse pulled up for me.

The nurse clucked as she checked over my head.

"You were right, you have a cut and a small bump, where it hit your head," she said as she placed a wet cold washcloth to the wound.

I winced as the cloth touched my head. The side of my head was definitely tender to the touch.

"I'll get you some ice. Do you want to stay here for a while?"

"No, I don't want to miss homeroom two days in a row. Can I take the ice with me?"

"Of course you can."

Sam and I said our goodbyes and headed out the door.

"Are you sure your head's okay?"

"Yeah, it only hurts if I touch it. What a jerk that guy was," I commented.

"Oh, you'll see many of those around here. Most of the students here were born with a silver spoon in their mouth, and are used to getting whatever they want. Having mommy and daddy bail them out of trouble is the norm. You and Mark will have to be careful. That guy was Matt Farrell, and he's a number one jerk. He seems to get a high out of messing with people. His dad's loaded, so he's used to getting his own way."

"Keeping our feelings secret seemed so simple this morning," I muttered as we walked through the classroom door.

The rest of the morning passed without anymore incidents, and even though I heard no more comments, I could still tell that many of the students were speculating about what had happened that morning.

Though I knew I should be concerned about what they were discussing, I was more anxious to see Mark again. Now that I knew who he was, and had spent part of the morning with him, I didn't like being separated from him at all. Which left me wondering how Sam felt not being with her guy all day? She had filled me in with a few sketchy details in-between classes on how she had been able to find her dream guy. I was able to glean the basics, like the fact that he was our age, but graduated early and was taking college courses. I intended to find out more after school.

The hours seemed to be going in slow motion as I waited for fifth period to arrive. In my head, I was mentally counting down the minutes and was relieved when fourth period ended.

Grabbing my stuff, I hurried off to meet Sam.

We both opted to eat inside, hoping to avoid another scene. We settled on a bench outside of the school library.

"How was fourth period?" Sam asked, as she unwrapped her tuna sandwich.

"It was fine. I was supposed to be reading, but I was too anxious to focus on the book. It's a good thing I'm a speed reader, or I would fall behind in class,"

Sam didn't have to ask me why I was anxious, she already knew. It was nice that we shared so many common bonds; it saved us from having to explain every little detail.

I took a big bite out of my own sandwich, just as the person I had been obsessing about all day walked around the corner. I sucked in a quick breath, causing the bite of sandwich to go down the wrong tube.

Coughing out of control, I reached for my bottle of water to try and wash the sandwich down and stop the coughing fit. Mark reached over, patting me on the back which made the situation worse. His touch flustered me; already choking, I could not handle losing the limited air I had in my lungs.

"I don't think she can breathe with you touching her," Sam commented, in a dry voice.

Mark looked at me. I confirmed Sam was right by a nod of my head.

"I'm Sam," she said, holding her hand out, giving me an opportunity to pull myself together.

I was disgusted with myself. So much for acting cool and collected, I thought as I wiped the tears from my eyes.

Mark reached out to shake Sam's hand. I could tell by the way he raised his eyebrows that he experienced the same connection with Sam as I did.

"I'm Mark, or for you, Mr. Russo for the next few months of school," Mark said with a smile.

I finally stopped choking like some idiot.

"Better now?" he asked with a twinkle in his eye.

I could tell that he liked the fact that he had such an impact on me. It wasn't like I could hide it though; just sitting by him had my heart racing to a tempo I was slowly getting used to.

"Will you meet me at the park after school?" he asked me in a more serious voice.

I felt warmed by his words. He acted like he wanted to be with me every bit as much as I needed to be with him.

"Yeah, I can meet you, but Sam has to come along too. That way it won't be a lie if I tell my mom I'm going to the park with Sam. You will just happen to be there," I said with a smile, as I found another loop hole in the need to know category.

"Is that okay with you?" I asked Sam.

"Sure, Shawn wants all of us to get together anyways."

"Who's Shawn?" Mark asked, momentarily confused.

"Sam's boyfriend; I mentioned him briefly to you this morning," I said subtly, reminding him that they had a lot in common with us.

"That's right," Mark said. "Well, I better head off to class," He reached out to brush back the hair that covered the lump on my head. He frowned when he saw my injury.

"That guy's lucky I'm an intern. I could have laid him out when I saw him chuck that softball at your head. It was all I could do to control myself. Does it hurt?" He inquired.

"No," I lied. Truth was it had been throbbing for most of the day.

I could tell that Mark saw right through my lie. He glanced down the hall to make sure we were alone and then bent over to press his lips against the bump.

Once again, my breath caught in my lungs. I was sure I would never breathe again. His lips erased all the pain, and instead warmth spread throughout every vein in my body.

By the time I could breathe again, he was gone.

"Wow! That was intense. I could feel the heat radiating off the two of you." Sam said, with laughter in her voice.

"Not to change the subject, but I have a question for you. Why did Matt call you *fridge* earlier?" I asked.

"Oh, it's a joke all the guys have. When I first moved here, a lot of them asked me out. I of course turned them down, so to cover up their bruised egos, they started calling me *frigid*, which eventually led to *fridge*. They're jerks. Even if I wasn't taken, I wouldn't give them the time of day," Sam said with disgust.

I agreed with her. All these years I had thought going to a private school would be great, but when you were surrounded by a bunch of spoiled people, it leaves a lot to be desired.

The bell rang as Sam and I gathered up our trash and threw it in the receptacle. I knew the next fifty minutes would be tough. Everyone in the class would be watching Mark and me to see if we *ogled* each other. I'm sure it would make their year if we made a spectacle of ourselves.

Sam and I grabbed the same seats we sat in the day before. I pulled out my notebook and sat ready to take notes. I felt everyone's eyes boring into me when Mark walked in the room. I kept my eyes firmly on the paper in front of me and thought of him as Mr. Russo.

He started right into the history lesson, and soon the scratching of pencils on paper could be heard throughout the room as all the students took notes on the day's lesson. He had an engaging voice and everyone was soon listening to him with rapt attention as he lectured about Europe during the turn of the century. If he ever decided to pursue a career in education, he would make an excellent teacher; even the gossip hounds were silent as he grabbed their attention with his warm voice.

He walked up and down the aisles as he lectured, and each time he passed me, my breath would catch and my heart would race. His voice soothed me like none had ever done before. I could have listened to him talk forever. His voice seemed to hold the nourishment my body craved.

Before I knew it, the bell rang. I finally looked up and met his eyes. I could tell the class had been just as tough for him.

He gave me a half smile as I gathered up my belongings. As Sam and I passed him, once again I felt him press something in my hand.

I did not open my hand until I left his classroom, but when I did, I saw another note and a small wrapped chocolate. I smiled. I had mentioned my addiction to chocolate during our morning talk. I placed the chocolate carefully in my bag.

Sam looked at me with interest.

I shrugged my shoulders. "I think I'll save it. It's the first thing he's ever given me," I said, feeling slightly self conscious.

I opened the note as Sam and I walked down the hall. There were only six words on the paper.

I can't wait to see you.

My palms grew sweaty. It was hard to believe that he liked me even though it was quite obvious just how ordinary I was. It would be one thing if I was as cute and bubbly as Sam. I felt a slight feeling of panic, wondering if he would change his mind.

The rest of the day passed quickly and I was pleased that I was at least able to concentrate more attentively on my afternoon classes than the day before. I would have hated to try to explain to my mom if my grades took a nosedive.

After the last bell rang, Sam and I both pulled out our cell phones to call our parents. I turned on my phone and saw that I had a voicemail from my mom. Hitting the button to retrieve the voicemail, I listened to the message.

"Hi, honey. I hope you don't mind. I heard there's an art seminar this afternoon in Aptos and I wanted to go check it out. I hate to abandon you two nights in a row. I promise we'll catch up tomorrow night. Call me if you have any problems."

Well, that worked out perfectly. No need to lie or find an alibi. I was free to meet Mark with no guilt. I felt giddy at my good fortune that we could spend the whole afternoon together.

"They said it was fine," Sam said as she dialed another number. She stepped away and I discreetly turned away to give her a little privacy.

"Shawn says he will meet us at the park."

"Great, let's go," I said in an impatient voice. I was ready to see Mark again. It had only been two hours, but I felt a small distinct ache from the separation.

We walked swiftly to the park.

Mark was already there sitting on the top of a picnic table under a big shady oak tree. It should be a sin to look as good as he did, I thought as I once again admired his physique.

He stood up as we approached.

"Hey Sam, how's it going?"

"Oh you know, my best friends dating our teacher's intern. I'm dating some guy I dreamt about my whole life and oh yeah, I share some kind of mystical connection with my friend and the intern," Sam quipped in a dry voice.

Mark and I burst out laughing.

Put that way, the whole situation seemed like some crazy story you would read about in the Enquirer. Sam was right, in the last thirty six hours our lives had taken a drastic turn.

A few minutes later, Sam's whole face lit up as she spotted someone walking toward us from the parking lot. She got up and practically bounced to his side, not bothering to even contain her enthusiasm. Sam gave him what I could only describe as a scorching kiss and then dragged him over to us.

"Krista, Mark, this is Shawn," Sam said with shining eyes.

I reached out to shake his hand. The now familiar electricity flowed between our hands. I was expecting it, but it was obviously a shock for Shawn.

"Wow," he said.

"Told you," Sam said, laughing at his expression.

He was expecting it when he shook Mark's hand, but it was clear that he was as confused as the rest of us over the bizarre situation.

For the next hour, we sat at the picnic table comparing stories. Shawn, like me, had been adopted at a young age. His adoptive parents split up five years ago, but he was fine about it. He felt his adoptive mom never wanted children and only went along with it to please his adoptive dad. "My adoptive dad was no gem," was all he said when I tried to ask him about it.

Out of the four of us, Mark was the only one who had been raised by his biological parent. We had no idea why, if we were all tied together in some way, why the rest of us had been abandoned.

Sam then filled Mark in on her past. She appeared to be glossing over a lot of the details, but we saw through them and I reached over to pat her hand. I already knew from small tidbits Sam had given me that her childhood had sucked. Eventually we ran out of steam and our conversation trailed off. We sat in silence for awhile analyzing all the information we lacked.

"I'm going to go read my book for awhile," Sam said. "I need a break from all this seriousness." She and Shawn got up and walked toward the jungle gym and climbed to the top.

Mark and I sat in silence. With Sam and Shawn gone I suddenly felt self-conscious. What if I couldn't think of anything intelligent to talk about? Sure, I had a high IQ, but I was way out of his league when it came to schooling, he was light years ahead of me. I studied the leaves that had fallen from the red oak trees that were scattered throughout the park. During all my research of California, I had seen that in parts of northern California, the trees grew so big and wide you could drive a car through them. My silent pondering was interrupted when Mark finally broke the silence.

"Do you want to take a walk around the park?" he asked. "It's bigger than it looks. There's a trail that wraps around back there, behind all the trees."

"Sure," I answered. He could have suggested walking to Florida, and I would have gladly followed him.

We set off following the trail. Mark reached over and grabbed my school bag with one hand, and my hand with the other. We walked in silence for a few minutes.

"Was my note too much?"

I stopped walking and turned to look at him.

"No, it all just seems to be happening so fast. I'm not sure what I feel, but I do know that I want to be with you all the time."

Relief covered his face. "I was afraid I was rushing you," he said as he pulled me into his arms.

Looking around, I could see that we were in the shadows of the trees and that it was hard to see more than a few feet in front of us. I could see that Mark was also aware of it. He pulled back slightly and cupped my face in his hands.

This was the moment I had been waiting for since I first laid eyes on him yesterday. That's not true, this was the moment I had been waiting for my whole life.

"So, you like to read?" He asked pulling away. I flushed when I realized he was standing a few paces away from me. I must have read the signals wrong; this is what I got for never hanging out with other people. I didn't even know when some guy was about to kiss me or not. *What a dork*, I thought, hoping he had missed the fawning look I was sure must have been on my face.

Swallowing the disappointment that was welled up in my throat, I tried to focus on the question he had asked me.

"Yeah, I love to read," I said, trying to inject some enthusiasm into my voice.

I found out that he liked to read as much as I did.

"Favorite book?" Mark asked.

"Easy, the sixth Harry Potter book."

"Really? More than the last Harry Potter book?"

"Definitely, the sixth book was the most interesting."

"How about you, what's your favorite book?"

"Well, like you, I like the Potter series, but I still like some of the classics like the *Outsiders* or *Where the Red Fern Grows*."

"Those books were banned from my house after I read them the first time," I said with a smile.

"Why?" Mark asked surprised.

"Because, I cried buckets after I read them, and walked around gloomy for weeks. After that, my dad would look at all my books before I read them to make sure no one died in them."

"How did you slide the Harry Potter books by him?"

"Well, those didn't turn sad until the last few. He screened the first couple, but after that he gave me free reign on them."

"Favorite food?" he asked, changing gears.

"Easy, chocolate," I said with a smile.

"Not favorite sweet, favorite substantial food?"

I laughed. "Chocolate is substantial."

Mark smiled also. "Okay favorite food after chocolate?'

"Hamburgers and fries," I said without hesitation.

"Junk food junkie, we're a match made in heaven."

"What's your favorite food?"

"Well, I like burgers and fries too, but I'm actually a pizza man. I love every kind of pizza imaginable. There's a great pizza place downtown that I'll take you to sometime."

I felt my pulse speed up at the thought of going out with him. Sure I was with him now, but the thought of actually going out on a date was exhilarating.

We continued to toss questions back and forth as the path weaved between the trees.

I found out that we both preferred cats over dogs, we liked the same comedies, and we both loved bike riding. He was the easiest person to talk to and we continued to talk as we looped the trail a second time. This time when we reached the shadows of the trees, I did not stop walking. It was obvious that he didn't want to kiss me. Maybe he was afraid he would be disappointed if he did, or maybe he was waiting for me to make the first move, I just couldn't tell. Though we didn't kiss, the conversation between us flowed easily, and we soon discovered that the connection shared between us during our dreams was even more prevalent in reality.

Chapter 6

The next few days passed in a blur. It was a novel thing to suddenly have three people to talk to that I felt so at ease with. My friendship with Sam was blooming, and my mom was amazed at how close we had become.

"You guys act like you've known each other your whole lives," she commented on Friday morning while we ate breakfast.

"She's just easy to talk to and we have so many things in common," I replied.

"Have you told her about your dreams?"She asked surprised.

"Um..." I was hoping she wouldn't ask that question.

The four of us had decided that we were going to keep our dreams between us. The idea that we had the same dreams seemed crazy enough to us, surely anyone else would think we were loony. None of us had any desire to wind up in a padded room.

"No," I mumbled, finally answering her question.

I hated lying to her, but I was doing what was best for her. I could already see the tension lines that had surrounded her eyes the last couple of weeks beginning to ease up. I knew a large part of this was because I was finally making friends, and of course she thought my bad dreams had gone away.

The dreams were still the same, but each morning when I woke from them, Mark would call me on my cell. We didn't talk about the dreams; instead, we would discuss other things, like our hopes and dreams. Neither of us were surprised that most of these were the same. It was as if he was the other half of me. By the time we hung up each morning, I was pretty much over the heartbreak of the dream, and when my mom woke, all signs of the dream were gone.

"So have the dreams changed?" my mom asked, as if she had peeked in my head and read my thoughts.

"Yeah, they're better now," I lied, finding no loop hole for this one.

"I better get ready for school," I said as I headed up the stairs. "Need to know," I chanted the overused words to myself.

Sam was waiting in the usual spot when mom pulled up to the school.

"Hi! Mrs. Miller," she called as I stepped out of the car adjusting my skirt.

"She's a sweet girl, you should ask her if she wants to come over for dinner tonight," she said as she waved at Sam.

"Okay. I'm sure she would like that; her parents are working on a big court case, and they've been stuck at the office late every night. I know Sam gets lonely by herself at night." Lying blatantly for the first time, I knew for a fact that Shawn spent all of his free time with Sam and I'm sure she was far from lonely.

"Why don't you see if she wants to stay over? Don't you have plans to get together tomorrow, anyways?" she asked.

"Yeah, we're going to the Boardwalk. Sam's a ride nut, and she wants to try the roller coaster."

Shawn and Mark were going with us too, but that obviously fell under the need to know category. Now that the newness of finding each other was beginning to fade, we were all anxious to figure out what tied us together. At first, I had felt apprehensive about going to such a public place, afraid we would run into students from school, but Mark and Sam both laughed at my concern.

"They wouldn't be caught dead at the Boardwalk. If it doesn't have the word country club or Gucci in it, they're not interested," Sam had said. "Most of them have houses on the beach and spend their weekends partying and drinking."

"I'll ask her. Thanks mom," I said, closing the door behind me.

Sam and I headed up the wide staircase leading into the school. After the incident on Tuesday, we were now in the habit of waiting for the bell to ring on the bench outside of the school library. We had dubbed it 'our spot,' and ate lunch there every day.

As we climbed the many stairs, I noticed Mark coming toward us. Even though I had talked to him just a few hours ago, I couldn't stop the excitement that raced through me at the sight of him. I drank in the sight of him and felt goose bumps pop up on my arms.

He nodded briefly to us as we passed as if we were just merely students. I wasn't hurt. We had kept our distance at school and the gossip about us had eased up. By Thursday, most students were busy gossiping about some poor sophomore who was gaining weight. Rumor had it, she was pregnant. I felt sorry for this unknown girl, but was relieved that the spotlight was off of us.

Though we pretended to be indifferent, we were both hyperaware of each other every second of the day. Every time I caught a glimpse of him throughout the day, my palms would sweat and my head would spin. Each time our eyes met it was like the first time. With each passing day we became more sensitive to each other's presence.

We continued to meet at the park every day after school and I felt like he knew me better than I did myself. There were no secrets between us. Each moment we were together was spent catching up on all the years we were unable to talk in the dreams. Sam and Shawn were always with us and made good chaperones. Not that they had anything to chaperone. Mark had yet to kiss me, and by Friday I was beginning to think he never would. Sure, he would touch my face or hold my hand, and each of these caresses always gave me the same warm feeling of familiarity that made my heart race, but I would give anything to feel his warm full lips on mine. I wanted to ask

Sam for her opinion, but was too embarrassed to admit that maybe Mark didn't want to kiss me.

Though we had all discussed it exhaustively, we were still no closer to figuring out the bond between the four of us. Sam and I had been surfing the web endlessly, searching for some link that would tie the four of us together. We found a few short articles related to my rescue when I was a toddler, but we were unable to gain any new information from the archives. Without the internet or amber alerts, the authorities had no luck locating my parents, and after a few months they had given up. Shawn and Sam had both wound up with the state, but Shawn, like me, had being adopted. Out of the four of us, Sam by far had it the worst. Not that you would have been able to tell, she was definitely the most upbeat one in our group. I think she was just glad to finally have people she cared about that felt the same way about her.

"So, my mom wants to know if you want to stay over tonight?" I asked Sam as we waited for the first bell to ring.

"Definitely, it will be my first sleepover."

"Mine too!" I quipped.

We both burst out laughing. We were nothing but a bunch of misfits. My mom was right; we acted like we were long lost sisters, which was one idea the four of us had discussed.

"No way," I had protested loudly. "I would know if I was related to you." I said looking at Mark.

"Not us," Mark stated. "I mean you and Sam. Maybe you're sisters or something like that."

"I thought about it," Sam said. "But our coloring and build are way off."

"Sam's right. I don't think we're related," I added. "The connection has to be something else."

"Is Mark meeting us at the park today?" Sam asked, breaking into my thoughts.

"No, not today," I answered with disappointment clouding my voice. "He has a staff meeting this afternoon. He said he would try to come over afterwards for awhile. My mom's going to an art show so it will be safe."

"Your mom's really taken to the art thing."

"Well, she hasn't started any projects yet, but she's definitely into learning about it," I replied with a laugh in my voice.

The bell rang.

Still laughing, we gathered up our books and walked down the busy hallway toward homeroom. We were both on a giggly high from the anticipation of our first sleepover. It felt good to be like a normal girl for once.

The morning classes passed quickly. We spent the time passing notes back and forth to each other. Getting good grades in school came naturally for both of us and neither of us had to pay much attention in class. We only bothered tuning into the lessons when we knew the teacher was watching us.

After lunch, we both headed off to history class. Though Sam was a good distraction, I was still keenly aware of every minute that passed until I would be with Mark again. My heart acted as an internal clock and every beat seemed to count the minutes for me.

When we entered the room, he was already there. I noticed that he was missing his usual smile. I looked at him questionably. He shook his head slightly. I sighed, *ugh*. This whole secrecy thing was becoming a big old pain in the butt. I hated waiting on things and hated surprises even more. The next hour stretched out endlessly ahead of me.

"What's up with him?" Sam whispered, leaning toward me.

I shrugged my shoulders, trying to act blasé about it. Something was obviously bothering him, but I would have to wait until later to find out, and we didn't want to give the gossip hounds anything new to talk about.

The next fifty minutes crawled by. I checked my watch almost every minute and it seemed to be moving backwards.

I gnawed on my thumbnail as I waited for class to end. Maybe he had decided to break off the relationship with me, and that was why he had not taken our relationship to the kissing stage.

Briiiiiiiiiing

"Finally!" I mumbled to Sam. "I never thought the class would end. I'm going to try to talk to him once everyone leaves the room."

I gathered my stuff slowly as I waited for the room to empty. Finally, the last student left the room.

I approached Mark, noting that he still wore the same grave expression.

"What's the matter?" I asked concerned.

"I had a meeting with the Dean this morning. It appears Matt followed up with his threat."

I gasped. "What did he tell him?" I asked, disgust rimming my voice.

"Well, Mr. Peterson asked me point blank if I was interested in a student. I couldn't lie to him. At first I was going to deny it, but I decided to come clean. He was unhappy with my answer, and expressed that was why he had qualms about letting me pursue my thesis here in the first place. He feels that the age gap between me and the students is too narrow. I tried to explain that it wasn't a problem, there was just something special about you."

"He didn't buy it. He gave me the whole, 'It's not professional to think about students that way.' The bottom line is, I'm supposed to stay away from you and finish my thesis up in a timely manner. He did tell me that he didn't feel comfortable writing me a letter of recommendation. Without a letter, it will be harder for me to get my thesis published." He ended his statement with a sigh.

I reached out a comforting hand.

"I'm so sorry," I said, feeling bad for the trouble I was causing him.

"So, we have to stay away from each other?" I said with a quiver in my voice. Just the thought of staying away from him sent my heart spinning in panic.

"*No*, he said he would *prefer* that I stay away from you. I would rather stop breathing than be away from you. My thesis is almost done anyway, I only needed to observe students' behavior's for a couple of weeks to gather enough data for my study. I should be done by next week and I don't think he's going to revoke my internship before I finish," he said, holding onto my hand.

My heart swelled as I comprehended his words. He wasn't breaking up with me. So what if we hadn't kissed yet, at least I wasn't losing him.

"You are the only thing that matters," he continued as he raised my hand to his chest and placed it over his heart. "Can't you feel what you do to me?" I could feel his heart racing under my palm. "It races like that anytime I'm near you, or anytime I think about you," he smiled. "Sam's right, we belong together, and nothing is going to keep us apart," he said with earnest.

I looked up into his eyes, he was right. When put like that, everything else seemed trivial. All that mattered is that we had found each other. The rest of the details, we could work out together.

I changed the subject.

"Will you still come over tonight? Sam's spending the night and we were going to search the Internet some more. Shawn will be coming over too for a little while.

"I'll be there as soon as the staff meeting ends. Do you want me to pick up some dinner?" he asked, handing me my customary chocolate.

"That would be great. I'm so excited it's Friday, and that we get to spend all day together tomorrow," I said. Throwing caution to the wind, I reached up and gave him a quick peck on the cheek. Before he could comment on the kiss, I sidled toward the door.

"I better go, the bells going to ring and I don't want to be tardy," I said in a hurry, feeling a little embarrassed over my impulsive act.

I did it, I kissed him; sure, not on the lips, but close enough. I closed the classroom door behind me, feeling a little smug from my bravery. Lost in thought, I was startled when I heard a voice behind me.

"Well, what did teacherpoo think about his talk with the Dean?" a snide voice asked behind me.

Turning around, I saw Matt leaning against the wall with an evil smile on his face. I was filled with an uncharacteristic urge to sock him, which was strange because I had always been the type to avoid any kind of conflict. Ever since I had met Mark and Sam, I just felt somewhat empowered and had more self-confidence. Still, I decided I would rather walk away than give this creep the satisfaction of seeing me upset.

I was jerked back as his hand wrapped around my left arm. He increased the pressure making me wince in pain. I didn't know what shocked me more-- the fact that he was touching me, or the pain. As a rule, I usually avoided contact with people to escape a rush from their emotions. Contact seemed to intensify the emotions someone was feeling, and Matt's negativity made my knees want to buckle.

"Not concerned? Maybe I will tell everyone you're a slut, he threatened. "Maybe that will put you in your place."

I felt heat overtaking my cheeks. My breathing became labored as I tried to fight back the flood of embarrassment. I knew I wasn't a slut, but I was shocked at the contempt in his voice. What had I done for him to obviously loathe me as much as he did?

I felt the sickness begin to spread and I knew from past experience, if I didn't sit down quick, the emotions would overtake me completely, and then I would embarrass myself further. Pulling back, I tried to jerk out of his hold, but he only tightened his fingers around my bicep making me gasp in pain.

"Please let go," I pleaded, closing my eyes to try to stop the sickness as it began to engulf me.

"Oof," I heard him grunt.

I felt his fingers slide off my arm; I opened my eyes in relief. I was shocked to find Matt on his knees in front of me. Mark was standing over him with a deadly look on his face. He had the fingers that had been pressed around my arm bent completely back.

"If you ever touch her again, I will kill you," he said in a quiet lethal voice. "If you even look at her, you will regret it, do you understand me?" To emphasize his point, he pushed Matt's fingers back even further.

Matt let out a whimper of pain.

Mark abruptly released his hold. "Get to class. *Now*," he threatened.

Matt got to his feet. With one last dirty look at both of us, he was gone.

Mark and I stood there for a moment. Then I felt the wave return, I knew I was going to be sick. I needed to get to a bathroom, and quick. Turning away, I fled, barely making it to the toilet before I retched horribly. Everything I ate that day insisted on coming up, until eventually, I was left heaving out nothing. When the wave passed, I rested my forehead on the side of the stall.

"What can I do?"

I cracked my eyes open. Oh God, he had followed me into the bathroom. I wanted to die of mortification. I didn't want him to see me like this.

"Water," I croaked.

"Okay, I'll be right back."

I rose on shaky legs and headed to the sink. Turning the cold water on, I cupped my hands and splashed water on my face. My cheeks were deep red and burned painfully.

"Did he hurt you?" Mark asked, as he handed me a bottle of water.

"No, I got sick because my emotions overtook me."

"Is it always like that?" he asked, concern now coloring his words.

"It used to be, but over the years I've learned how to control it. This was different; it was a combination of feelings. I was embarrassed, scared, and very angry. Plus, because he was touching me, I got to deal with all of his loathing feelings. When I have that many emotions, it's hard to fight back the sickness," I said weakly. My body felt like it had gone through a ringer.

Mark lightly grabbed onto my elbow and guided me down the hall to an unused classroom. He helped me to a desk and sat across from me with concern still etched on his face.

"Are you sure you're okay?" he asked, rubbing the side of my face. "Do you need anything else?"

I rested my pounding head against the palm of his hand. His touch was instantly soothing and the pounding receded to a dull throb.

"He's going to go to the Dean," I muttered.

"No, I don't think he will. He doesn't want to look like a weakling. He's not going to admit to anyone that I got the better of him. He may try to get revenge in one way or another, but I'm pretty sure he is smart enough to stay away from you from now on."

"I've never seen anyone look at someone with such menace. You looked like you could have killed him."

"I wanted to. It was all I could do to control my rage. I have never felt that way. I can't explain what it did to me to see his hands on you and to hear you pleading for him to let you go," he said.

I could still feel the anger radiating off of him. I placed my hands on his face to soothe him. After a moment, I could feel the tension sliding away from his body. And with one last shudder, the last of his anger left as I dropped my hands.

"It's a good thing I don't have a sixth period class," he said as he settled back in his chair. Looking down, he used the edge of his thumbnail to scrape an old piece of tape off the side of the desk.

I watched him silently for a few moments, sensing he was embarrassed by his reaction to Matt. I should have felt angry that Mark had resorted to violence. I had always been against any kind of violence and had always shied away from it. But I wasn't, I felt Matt deserved it and was touched by the intensity of Mark's emotions for me.

"I don't feel like heading to class, I think I'm going to tell the school nurse I'm sick. I'll wait for Sam at the park. Will you tell her for me?" I asked him.

"Sure, I'll send a note to her seventh period class. Do you want me to walk you over?"

"No, I think we've caused enough trouble today, we don't want to push the Dean any further."

Mark held out his hand to help me out of my chair. Once I was on my feet, he pulled me in his arms.

"I'm sorry you got so sick."

"It comes with the territory, I'm just sorry you had to watch," I grimaced, thinking that he had definitely seen me at my worse. Nothing was grosser than watching someone throw-up.

"I've got to head back to class. Mr. Jackson wants me to go into more detail about the concentration camps and the role the Nazis had in them. I'll meet you at your house after my meeting," he said as he leaned down to peck me on the cheek.

I raised my hand to my cheek after he left the room. My skin tingled where his lips had touched me. I paused a moment to catch my breath and tried to gather my thoughts. Maybe my peck earlier had given him a push in the right direction.

I got the okay to go home from the school nurse and walked the half a block to the park, slowly taking in my surroundings as I walked. I loved seeing so much color; exotic flowers bloomed everywhere I looked. Back home spring would be on its way, but up north it was always a little slow to begin. Here, it already looked like the middle of summer. I watched as two birds fought over the same tasty treat on one of the lawns and smiled when the smaller one came out the victor.

By the time I reached the park, my depleted energy was obvious and I gratefully settled on a low park bench that sat directly in the sun. I knew the heat from the sun would chase away the chills that always followed a bad episode.

With drowsy eyes I watched the only occupants at the park. Most were young mothers who were chasing after their small toddlers. By the squeals of delight they gave out each time they were caught, this was obviously a favorite game.

I smiled as I rested my head back and closed my eyes. The sun felt wonderful beating down on my face. The sounds of the children faded away, as I slipped into a nice peaceful slumber.

I dreamed about him. Not the usual dream where we stood on our beach, but a more personal one where we were kissing. The dream was so real; I could feel the heat of his breath as he fanned kisses across the plains of my face. Each kiss left just the slightest bit of electricity across my face where his lips had touched. I felt warmth spreading up through my toes and expanding through all my limbs.

I opened my eyes and saw the object of my fantasy sitting beside me.

I flushed slightly. Could he tell that I had been dreaming about him kissing me? It was a surreal feeling to be dreaming about him one moment, only to awaken with him beside me.

I sat up straighter, but grimaced when I felt a pinch in my neck from being in one position too long. Glancing at my watch, I was surprised to see that school was over.

"I thought you had a meeting?"

"I do. I just walked Sam over. I wanted to check on you before I headed to the meeting."

At his words, I noticed Sam standing to the side for the first time. Her face was clouded over.

"What's wrong?" I asked.

"It must have been pretty bad if you threw up," Sam said.

"What do you mean? Krista said throwing up is normal," Mark interrupted.

I pleaded with Sam with my eyes to drop it.

Sam ignored my silent plea and plunged on. "He has to know Krista," Sam said. "We made a pact that we would share everything. We're never going to figure out the connection if we keep things from each other."

I knew she was right. We could have no secrets, but I also didn't want him worrying about me unnecessarily.

"We only throw-up when our emotions are completely out of control, and usually only when we're scared. Trust me, growing up I threw-up many times from fear. Matt must have scared Krista a lot for her to get so sick," Sam added.

"Is that true?" Mark demanded.

"Yeah," I mumbled, "When I was younger, my parents sheltered me a lot when they figured out how sensitive I was. They found out early on, it was worse when I was scared. So, they made sure I was never frightened. I wasn't expecting him to grab onto me, and it startled me. I didn't mean to deceive you, you just seemed so mad already. I didn't want to add to it."

"You can't keep things from me. You have to trust me with everything," Mark said quietly. "Are you feeling better now?"

"Yes, the heat from the sun and the nap gave me back my strength,"

Mark glanced at his watch, swearing softly as he stood up. "I have to go, but we're going to talk about this again later."

He turned to Sam, "Did you call your foster mom?"

"Yes, she's on her way. She went home and packed an overnight bag for me. She said she would give us a ride to Krista's house."

"Good," he said.

"I'll see you both in awhile; make sure she takes it easy until I get there," he told Sam as he turned and walked away.

After he left, Sam sat down next to me. "Are you mad at me?" she asked, gnawing on the inside of her lip.

I shook my head. "I should have told him the truth earlier, but I thought he would kill Matt. I have never seen someone so mad before. It was radiating off of him. Matt could feel it also. I could tell he was scared of Mark. To tell you the truth, I was glad he was scared, now maybe he will leave us alone."

107

Beeeeep!

Sam and I looked up.

"Oh, there's my foster mom."

We both grabbed our school bags and headed toward the sleek BMW that was idling at the curb. Sam opened the car door and introduced me.

"Krista, this is Karen, my foster mom. Mom, this is Krista."

"It's a pleasure to meet you Krista, thanks for keeping our girl company this past week. My husband and I have been up to our eyeballs in the case we're handling. I can't wait until the trial is over. Once it is, we can return the favor and you can stay overnight. Sam has talked about you non-stop and we're so happy you moved here."

"I am too," I said as I settled into the plush leather seats of the BMW. Boy, their car made ours look like a matchbox car, I thought as I inhaled the rich smell of the leather seats. "Otherwise, Sam and I would have never met," I continued on.

"She's a special girl and we're glad you're friends."

Sam flushed at Karen's words. I couldn't help wondering if compliments about her had been few and far between growing up. Were these foster parents the first to ever show any interest in her?

I felt an unfamiliar feeling of anger well up inside me. Why did parents abandon their children? Did they not care about the life they were condemning their children to? Sure, I had lucked out, but what about poor Sam.

Karen pulled her car up in front of my house. Sam and I piled out while Karen popped the trunk open so Sam could grab her overnight bag. She handed Sam some money and told her to have a good time.

Chapter 7

We stowed Sam's bags on the floor in my room before we headed back to the sitting room to listen to music. I turned the volume down so I could fill Sam in on what she had missed.

"So, what's the Dean going to do?" Sam asked after she heard all the details.

"Mark's not sure, he's on some kind of probation and if word gets out about what he did to Matt, I'm sure the Dean would discontinue his study. We need to be careful over the next few months. I don't want to ruin his whole career."

"That Matt's a snake," Sam muttered. "I wish I could have seen the look on his face when Mark grabbed his hand."

For the first time since it had happened, I could smile and appreciate the fact that Matt had gotten a taste of his own medicine for once.

"You've got a point. You should have seen the look on his face. I thought he was going to wet his pants."

Both of us burst out laughing at the thought of Matt walking through the hall with wet pants. The *Lush Trio* wouldn't think he was so hot then.

"I don't see Matt letting this slide," Sam said, sobering both of us up.

"I know. He can't be trusted."

"So, your foster mom seems nice." I said, changing the subject.

"Yeah, they're both nice; I lucked out when they placed me with them. They act like they like me or something."

"They do like you, you're easy to like. All your other foster parents were just too stupid to realize it," I stated.

Embarrassed by the compliment, Sam stood up and started browsing through the books that lined the shelves. I turned up the music and picked up my current book, giving Sam privacy to digest the compliment. Sam selected a book and settled into the chair next to me.

I peeked over at Sam whose cheeks were still slightly flushed; I looked down and began to read my own book. We sat in compatible silence. After a while, Sam looked up. "I'm glad we're friends," she said simply.

"I am too."

We smiled at each other, in what I'm sure others would have called a *cheesy* kind of way. The time passed swiftly and before we knew it, Mark and Shawn were there with dinner.

Sam and I bounded downstairs to open the front door for them with the same cheesy smiles on our faces from before. It should be sin to be as happy as we were.

"Hi!" we said, greeting them in unison as they stepped over the threshold. I smiled brilliantly at Mark as he closed the door behind him.

"Boy, you seem to be feeling better," he observed.

"I do! Sam and I have been vegging out all afternoon."

"I'm glad. I picked up burgers and fries for dinner. I hope that's okay?" He asked holding up a beautifully greasy brown bag.

"That's perfect, I love fast food," I said, acting like he didn't already know.

He laughed.

"You and Sam can go upstairs. I'll grab some plates and some sodas," I said to Shawn. Shawn and I hadn't done a whole lot of talking, and I still felt a little self conscious around him. Usually, Sam monopolized the conversation, or the guys would converse amongst themselves. They had spent hours philosophizing how we all managed to wind up together here. They had theories that ranged from mystical to science fiction, but it was hard to think of any reason that didn't sound completely ridiculous to me.

Mark and I headed to the kitchen and grabbed some paper plates, napkins, and sodas. We could hear the easy bantering between Shawn and Sam as we carried everything up to my loft. It seemed so strange to have so many people over. Growing up, my parents had lots of friends, but they usually hung out at their houses so I wouldn't be uncomfortable around them. For the most part, it had always been us three, and then when my dad passed it away, it was just the two of us.

112

The four of us chatted while we filled up on junk food. We never seemed to run out of topics. We all have IQ's that are higher than average, and we discovered that we have read many of the same books. Although, Shawn's taste ran a little more toward sci-fi and Mark's seemed more mystical, (which is how we wound up with the wide spectrum of theories). Sam and I were both diehard romantics, and loved many of the same classics.

After we were done eating, I grabbed my laptop and booted it up. While the computer was warming up, Mark pulled out the small notebook we were using to write down the connections we all shared.

I read over his shoulder as he added all the same books we had all read to the list. Sam and I named off others he had forgotten.

"I made a list of more websites for us to check out," he said. "I think we should Google the name 'Franklin,' and see what comes up. All this time I thought Franklin was the guy's name, but now I'm wondering if that's a cover. It bothers me that Krista mentioned 'Franklin' to the authorities, but couldn't remember her mom or dads name," he said.

"Well, she was only two," Sam piped in.

"Yeah, but I think most two-year-olds can say their own name. We all know we're smarter than average. So, how come most two-year-olds can tell you their parent's names, but Krista couldn't? Doesn't that strike you as weird?" he asked. "I can't help wondering if she was separated from her parents a long time before this 'Franklin' person dropped her off."

"I thought we already decided that this whole thing is weird," Sam piped in once again.

I settled on the floor with Sam and Mark on each side of me, while Shawn settled into the lazy-boy across from us. I clicked on the Internet icon and soon we were surfing the web. Technology is a wonderful thing.

I typed in the name 'Franklin' on the Google screen. We could see that the list that popped up was endless and had multiple pages. I used the mouse to scroll down the list. Mark wrote down some that might be helpful. The first one on his list was for a trucking company named 'Franklin and Sons.' We all decided it made sense. Maybe a trucker dropped me off and used the name on the side of the truck. We all mulled it over, it seemed plausible.

I clicked onto the 'Franklin and Sons' website. It opened to a full page ad that had a big semi-truck on it. I clicked the icon that showed the history of the company. We were all disappointed when we read that the company was founded only five years ago by a man and his two sons.

"Well there goes that idea," Sam commented.

I exited out of that page and went back to the listings for *Franklin*. The next one on the list was for a pharmaceutical company. We discarded that one and moved on down the list. We searched for over an hour, but no other websites panned out. Finally giving up, I switched off the computer.

"I need another soda," Sam said, rising from her spot on the floor. "Does anyone else need anything?"

"I do," Mark and I both said in unison.

"I'll go with you," Shawn said as we all laughed.

Shawn grabbed Sam's hand and gave her a quick but searing kiss before he led her down the stairs. I couldn't help the shot of envy that sliced through me. I envied the ease they had. They seemed to know exactly what the other wanted and they were so attuned to each other, it was like watching an old couple waltz on the dance floor for the millionth time. They seemed aware of every move the other was going to make. I couldn't help thinking despairingly that maybe Mark and I were not as good a fit as they were.

I set the computer off to the side and turned to face Mark and saw that he was staring at me intently. My pulse sped up when he reached over and twirled a lock of my hair around his finger.

"You are so beautiful. I've seen you hundreds of times in my dreams over the years, but they never did you justice," he said, as if he sensed my insecurities.

My breath came out in small shallow gasps as we stared intently at each other. Was this the moment I had waited for, was he finally going to kiss me? My palms began to sweat.

I closed my eyes as he slowly leaned toward me.

My eyes sprung open at the sound of Sam and Shawn bounding up the stairs.

"Oops sorry, I didn't mean to interrupt," Sam said flushing a dull pink.

Swallowing my disappointment, I heard Mark let out a small groan of frustration. I felt my heart lighten. Well, at least it seems like he wanted to kiss me this time, I thought to myself.

Mark stood up. "We better head out," he said to Shawn. "We'll meet you guys tomorrow at the Boardwalk."

I stood up also. "That sounds perfect. My mom said I could borrow the car all day. She's finally going to start painting tomorrow, so she's looking forward to having the house to herself."

Sam and I walked the guys down the stairs. Sam followed Shawn out the front door and walked him to the car probably trying to give us privacy for interrupting us upstairs. Mark missed the hint though and only paused briefly; he used his palm to cup my face, but instead of kissing me, he gently rubbed his thumb over my bottom lip. I shivered from the contact and felt goose bumps pop up along my arms. Holy cow, if kissing him felt half as good as this, I knew I was a goner.

"I'll see you later," he said.

I smiled a little sadly. We both knew in just a few short hours we would be with each other in our *dream world*, and even though the dreams had taken a painful twist, neither one of us would give them up for anything.

My mom arrived home just minutes after Mark and Shawn left. I couldn't help breathing a sigh of relief that the timing had worked out. I just wasn't ready to cross that bridge and introduce Mark to her yet.

"Hey girls, how was your evening?" My mom inquired, setting her overflowing bags on the settee that was against the wall just past the front door.

"It was fun." Sam and I burst out laughing as we answered at the same time again. We were like two halves that had been put back together.

My mom smiled at our light hearted mood. "Do you girls have any interest in playing games with an old lady for a little while?"

"Mom, you're not an old lady," I protested, standing up to get some games.

"Ugh." I groaned dismayed, as I began the search for a deck of cards that was buried somewhere within a cluster of games spilling off the overflowing shelves. How the closet had gotten this bad when we only had been in the new house for a few short weeks was beyond me. I lifted the Monopoly and Pictionary games out of the way and caught the Scrabble board as it slid out of its torn box. Finally, I spied the cards shoved all the way in the back. Juggling the games with one hand, I plunged my free hand toward the back of the shelf and groped around for the cards, praying silently that my hand wouldn't encounter any creepy crawlies. I detested bugs and usually strayed away from placing my hand into dark corners.

We decided to play rummy since Sam had never played it before. Mom briefly explained the rules to Sam while I forged into the kitchen to make all of us hot fudge sundaes.

Sam kept us in stitches while we played the game; she had a hard time remembering the rules, so she made up her own. We laughed at her outrageous rules and soon we were all making up our own rules. We played cards late into the night, laughing and joking around.

117

Finally, my mom yawned and announced it was way past her bedtime. Sam and I were still hyped up from the ice cream, so we continued our game upstairs. We sat on my bed for another hour gossiping, while we played.

By 1:00 a.m. our sugar rush had disappeared and we were ready to turn in. I put the cards away and pulled out my trundle bed for Sam while she used the bathroom. When Sam was done, I shuffled to the bathroom; I washed my face and brushed my teeth. As I reached over to switch off the light, I caught a glimpse of my reflection and was amazed at the differences. I barely recognized the smiling girl who looked back at me. Mark and Sam had changed my life. The seriousness that had always circled my eyes was now replaced by laugh lines.

I crawled in bed and switched off the lamp, mumbling a goodnight to Sam and within minutes we were out.

My sobs woke both of us up an hour later.

Sam got up and sat beside me. I felt comfort flow through me just by her presence.

"Was it the same?" she asked quietly.

I nodded my head. "Yeah, it hasn't changed. It just seems that with each passing night the pain from the separation has gotten more intense. I don't understand why we're going through this and you and Shawn never have."

"I don't know," Sam said with sympathy, but I could tell she was relieved she had never experienced it. Shawn and Sam's relationship was not as complicated as Mark and mine. They had known who the other was almost instantly when Sam had run into him while he was working at the Boardwalk. She of course had never seen his features, but she had embraced her *lighting moment*, and believed Shawn the instant he told her who he was. Their dreams had never taken the turn that Mark and mine were on, so Mark's theory that ours had changed because of the move didn't seem feasible now.

I was interrupted from my thoughts by the buzzing of my cell phone. I glanced at the caller I.D. already knowing who it was.

"Are you okay?" he asked as soon as I answered the phone.

"Yeah, it's just getting harder each time."

"For me too."

"I'm glad you called, Sam and I were just going over it."

"I'm glad she's there with you, I worry about you after the dream ends each night."

"I'm okay. I just wish I knew why our dreams have changed and theirs haven't. We're all looking for what ties us together, but the more we get torn apart, the less likely it seems," I said as Sam got up to use the bathroom. I felt a small guilty twinge; I knew that Mark and my dream twist stressed her out. I didn't want her to think I was wishing the cruel twist on them, it just felt grossly unfair to me.

We talked for a few more minutes until I started to yawn and began to feel drowsy. My body needed rest after the emotional upheaval it had suffered throughout the day.

"I'll let you go," Mark said as I stifled another yawn. "I'm picking Shawn up, and we will meet you and Sam by the entrance."

"Okay," I said, dying to say the three little words chanting in my head. "Sleep well," I said, chickening out at the last second.

Chapter 8

I woke with Feline lying on my face. Pushing him off gently, I sat up and looked over at Sam who was snoring softly on the trundle bed beside me. I was glad to see that she was able to go back to sleep after I had woken us both up with my dream.

I wasn't as lucky. I had badly wanted to see nothing but darkness when I closed my eyes, but instead was flooded with the images of Mark being pulled away yet again. I had hoped that since Mark and I were growing so close, that the bad turn the dreams had taken would have stopped, but actually they were getting worse. It always feels like Mark is taken against his will, but maybe that's just me being naïve. Of course the torment that has shackled me my entire life from being abandoned by my real parents didn't help; add to that the grief from my adoptive father dying, and all I could think was that maybe I was cursed somehow, and doomed to spend my life alone.

Since sleep was no longer an option, I decided to quietly get up, taking care not to wake Sam. The sun was just beginning to rise as a soft pink hue crept through my blinds. Feline left the room with me and waited for me to settle in one of the chairs in my loft area before he leaped onto my lap. I stroked his soft fur absently. It seemed selfish to feel so melancholy when I had literally met the guy of my dreams. I should be jumping for joy at my good fortune, but instead I was filled with doubts about the stableness of our relationship in light of the dreams. Could the dreams really mean that he was going to leave me? Maybe I just wasn't what he was expecting after dreaming about me for so long. Maybe I should break it off to protect my heart before it was too late? Just the thought of ending it left me cold. It was way too late for that now. I loved him; I have always loved him, I just had to trust my heart that he loved me also.

Frustrated that I was ruining a day I had been looking forward to, I set Feline on the floor and headed off to the bathroom to take my shower. I showered quickly and within minutes I was blow drying my hair. Instead of my usual ponytail, I opted to pin the sides back with a couple of bobby pins. I added a dab of foundation and a touch of peach lip gloss to my dry lips. With one last glance in the mirror, I switched off the light and headed back to my room to wake up Sam.

She was already up. I recognized the small secretive smile on her face that I myself had worn hundreds of times over the years before my own dreams had taken their sudden dark turn. It was the smile of just waking up from a dream where you had been with the guy you love all night.

"Is it okay if I go take a shower?" She asked.

"Of course, you never have to ask, what's mine is yours."

I took a few minutes to straighten up the clutter from our late night. I made my bed and folded Sam's blankets before stowing the trundle bed away. I clicked on my IPod and scrolled down to my favorite play list and then docked it on my stereo. Music flowed out of the speakers and I danced down the stairs with Feline once again at my heels.

I popped a couple of whole grain bagels into the toaster and grabbed the cream cheese and OJ from the fridge. While I waited for our breakfast to finish, I filled Feline's food and water dish and poured two tall glasses of juice.

The bagels popped up and I reached for them without thinking, burning my fingers on the hot metal on the side of the toaster. A few choice curse words ran through my head in quick succession as I stuck my throbbing fingers into my mouth and sucked on them as I struggled to open the freezer door with one hand. Right about now, I missed the fridge with the automatic ice dispenser from our old house. I pulled the ice tray out with my good hand and made the futile attempt to disengage the ice from the plastic holder one handed. Giving up in frustration, I struck the edge of the laminate counter with the plastic ice tray sending four cubes scattering across the kitchen. One bounced into the sink, another skidded across the floor landing under the ancient stove, and two slid across the counter. I rescued the two on the counter, wrapped them in the middle of a paper towel, and placed them on my still throbbing fingers looking for relief.

I did the best I could, gingerly spreading the cream cheese on the bagels. "None of this would have happened if I was eating a cupcake," I muttered to Feline. I hated the days that I had to eat healthy. A brownie would have hit the spot this morning and I wouldn't have burned the tips of my fingers like an idiot. I scowled when I saw the angry blisters that had risen on three of my fingers. "Great I look like a mutant freak."

I headed back upstairs juggling the bagels and OJ for each of us and heard the shower click off as I set the plates and glasses on the table.

My mood lightened when I realized that in a few hours I would be with Mark again. The other stuff I would work out later. For now, I just wanted to be with him at whatever cost, even if it meant another blow to my fragile heart.

After breakfast, we finished cleaning up and then headed downstairs. I walked to my mom's studio at the back of the house and tapped on the door quietly.

"Come in," my mom called out.

"So, you guys are off?"

"Yeah, we ate breakfast and now Sam's ready to tackle some rides. Do you think I can have some money for the day?"

"I left a couple of twenties on the counter for you. Be careful and stay together," she said as I headed out the door.

I grabbed the car keys and the money my mom left out for me, and Sam and I headed out the door.

We rolled the windows down and cranked the music up as we drove to the Boardwalk. We couldn't help but belt out the words to the music as the warm sea air ripped into the car blowing through our hair. I sniffed in appreciation. The smell of the ocean was definitely one thing that I loved about living here.

Mark and Shawn were waiting for us by the entrance as promised, and my doubts were put to rest as I gazed at him. What had I been thinking? There was no way I could ever let him go. If he ever decided to leave me, I would just to have to deal with it, but for now, I was going to live in the moment. I had spent my whole life so far over analyzing every decision. This time I would let my heart lead the way.

Mark and I slowly followed behind Sam and Shawn as we quietly talked about our dream from the previous night.

"What do you think it means?" I finally asked after a few seconds of silence.

"I don't know, but we should definitely be on guard, I'm not happy about the alteration of our dreams, and all the other things that are going on. It's cool that we all share some kind of bond, but I'm concerned about the ramifications of what it all means."

"I am too. I'm scared you're going to leave me," I admitted in a quiet voice.

Looking down, I wished I could retract the words, but they were already out there. What was wrong with me? I had always been such a private person, and here I was spilling out my darkest insecurities with the one person that I wanted to keep them from.

Mark reached out and grabbed onto my hand, lending me the reassurance that he was here now. We walked hand in hand behind Shawn and Sam who was practically bouncing with excitement over the rides. She was like a kid on her way to meet Santa. Her excitement was contagious and mine and Mark's somber mood were lifted as we watched her.

The first ride Sam wanted to go on was enough to make my head spin just looking at it. The attendant helped us into the car after high-fiving Shawn.

"Hey man, what's up? You don't get enough of this place when you're on duty?" Shawn laughed. "What can I say, I'm a glutton for punishment," he said as his friend closed the door to our car.

Before I knew it, we were spinning out of control. Sam gripped the steering wheel in the middle of the car and increased the spinning even more. The momentum of the spinning sent me crashing against Mark's rock hard side. I gasped in awareness as my body touched his from shoulder to toe.

Sam laughed at me as I staggered off the ride like I was drunk. Of course little did Sam know, it had nothing to do with the ride. I chanced a look at Mark and was surprised that he looked like he was suffering from a case of vertigo also.

"Boy you guys are lightweights. That ride was nothing," Sam said, laughing at us.

By the knowing look on Shawn's face, he knew that it wasn't the ride that had messed with Mark and me.

I felt my face begin to heat up. Instead of answering Sam, I followed meekly behind her as she dragged us toward the next ride. The next ride must be one of the favorites at the park if the long line was any indication. Shawn used his connections to get us to the front of the line.

Sam cracked up at the disgruntled mumbling of those waiting in line. "This is so cool," she squealed. "I feel like a V.I.P."

We chattered about mundane things while we were walking to the front of the line. I studied the ground under my feet as we walked to conceal my continuing embarrassment from before. Sam seemed oblivious to anything and kept the conversation flowing.

"Have you been on this ride before?" I asked Mark, finally able to look at him without fearing I would embarrass myself again.

"Sure, lots of times. Like Sam, I'm kind of a speed freak."

At his words, I started to question the sanity of riding the roller coaster. High speed acceleration did not sound like something I wanted to try. I searched my head trying to come up with a valid excuse to skip the ride, but not wanting to look like a wimp, I saw no way out.

Sam's excitement grew as we boarded our cars. I felt my heart jump to my throat when I saw the steep incline, followed by the even sharper decline. The roaring sound of the cars combined with the screaming riders as they rocketed by was enough to make my forehead bead with sweat. There is no way I can do this, I thought to myself.

The others seemed unaware of my inner torment as they compared notes on the wildest rides they had been on. I looked at them like they were speaking a foreign language.

I shifted in my seat; it was now or never, if I didn't say something quick, I would be stuck riding. Mark reached for my hand as we sat in our seats. His touch was as soothing as ever and most of my nervousness faded away. Maybe I could do it. The ride wasn't that long; if I kept my eyes closed, it would be over before I knew it. *Then he will never know what a wimp you can be*, I thought. I gripped his hand tightly as another attendant came by lowering the lap bar. My palms started to sweat and my legs started to shake from nerves as the lap bar was lowered over us. Finally sensing my dread, Mark reached over and placed a strong arm around me, pulling me tightly against his side. He placed his other hand on my knee to calm my quaking and leaned over and whispered in my ear.

"I'm sorry, I didn't realize rides scare you," he said softly.

"I'm not scared I'm just really..."

As the ride began to move forward, I blanched realizing there was no turning back now. Mark pulled me even closer, whispering in my ear. Sam turned and looked at us as the ride picked up speed. She looked at me questioningly, but I stared right through her. The car picked up speed and before we turned the first bend, Sam looked like she was trying to ask me something, but I heard nothing as the roller coaster started its slow chugging climb to the top of the first drop.

I couldn't remember a time that I was as terrified as I was at this moment. I had never admired kids that buckled under peer pressure, but here I was a victim of myself. I squeezed my eyes closed and gripped Mark's hand on my knee. The emotions I was feeling were just another downfall to being oversensitive. Luckily, Mark's touch distracted me enough that I was no longer sure if my heart was beating wildly form the ride, or the fact that his hand was on my knee. The ride was over within seconds and I was proud of myself for not throwing up.

"You made it," Mark whispered in my ear. I turned my face and felt his lips graze my cheek. My knees started trembling again and it had nothing to do with the ride.

"What should we go on next?" Sam asked as she bounced along beside us.

"I'm out." I said finally, deciding not to be a follower.

"What? Are you kidding?" Sam asked, like I was nuts.

"You guys can go on whatever you want, but these kinds of rides scare me," I said with more conviction than I felt.

"We should take a break anyways," Mark interjected before Sam could protest. "Besides, we're really here for another reason," he said, looking pointedly at the beach in front of us.

"Oh yeah, I guess I got caught up in the moment," she said, grabbing onto Shawn's hand.

We had all decided that the best starting point for figuring out what tied us together was to go to where it all seemed to have started. We needed to see how we would all feel being on the beach together.

Mark and I walked a few paces behind Sam and Shawn as we headed toward the concrete stairs that would lead us to the beach. I could hear Sam's excited chatter, but could not distinguish the words.

We all paused about 10 feet past the concrete wall. There was no mistaking the surge of electricity that seemed to shoot up through the sand and into our bodies. I looked at the astonishment on the other's faces and knew I was wearing the same expression on mine.

"This is insane," I mumbled to Mark.

"This whole week has been insane. First, we find out that the people we have dreamed about our entire lives really exist, and then we all end up in the same city, at the same time."

Mark's words did little to soothe me.

What other surprises could we possibly discover? I thought to myself as I removed my flip flops.

"I have something I want to show you," Shawn piped in. "I was waiting until we were all here together, at this spot. It's a picture I've had since I was little. Sam has already seen it," Shawn said, revealing yet another surprise.

My thoughts were interrupted by Mark. "What's so special about the picture and why did you want us to see it here?" He asked.

"See for yourself," Shawn said, digging around in his knapsack. Shuffling clothes and toiletries around, he finally extracted a big yellow manila envelope. Pulling the tabs open, he carefully removed an object covered in bubble wrap. He gently peeled the wrapping away to reveal a plastic Ziploc baggie with a faded worn picture inside.

"I put it in a baggie a few years ago after I discovered that my constant handling was ruining it. I knew it was important to preserve it the best I could," he said as he gingerly handed the picture over to Mark.

Mark reached out to take the picture. Curiously, I looked over his shoulder to see what would make him treat it like it was some kind of crown jewel. I gasped when I saw the picture.

It appeared to have been taken exactly where we were standing, with the same Boardwalk in the background. There were four couples standing side by side. They all looked relatively happy and the women were obviously very pregnant, judging by the size of their bellies. At their feet were four little boys that appeared to be about one year old. They looked so care-free, digging in the sand with brightly colored shovels.

"Why are you showing us this now when...?" Mark said in a voice laced with anger.

I could relate to his feelings. We had spent the entire week trying to find something that linked us together and Shawn had this picture the entire time.

"Look, don't be mad," Shawn said, interrupting Mark's tirade before he could build steam. "I wanted to make sure you guys felt the same pull to this place as Sam and I. Sam wanted me to show you earlier this week, but I had to be sure that we were all really connected."

"Shawn thinks they might be our parents," Sam said in a quiet voice.

I swallowed an unexpected lump in my throat as I grabbed the picture from Mark's hand and critically studied it. Could Sam be right? Were these our parents? They don't look like the type of parents that would abandon their children, I thought to

131

myself. As a matter fact, the way they rested their hands on their bellies conveyed a feeling of love for the unborn babies they carried.

"Well your right about that," Mark said with certainty. "That's my dad, and I recognize the picture of my mom from a picture I saw a few years back in my dad's desk drawer. I was going to ask him for the picture, but never worked up the nerve because I know he doesn't like to talk about her."

I started to feel a wave of unease approach, but I quickly stifled it the best I could before it became an issue.

After a few minutes of silence, I finally asked the obvious question that they were all struggling with. "Why are we all drawn here?" I asked, spreading out my arms.

"I don't know, but I want to know what the connection is with this place. What happened here to make all of us feel the need to be here?" Mark answered.

"Your forgetting something else that is important?" Sam said.

"What's that?"

"Look at the couples, there's four of them with four little boys and four babies on the way."

Understanding dawned on me. Sam raised a valid point. Only four of us were standing here now. Which meant, somewhere out there were four more people that could be just like us. Maybe the others in the picture were normal, but it seemed highly unlikely. Some force connected all of us, and it had started here.

"I think we need to do some research and find out if anything happened on this beach eighteen or so years ago," Shawn said.

"Like what? A UFO sighting? That's crazy," I said.

"All of this is crazy, but if not UFO's, then maybe something else paranormal. Or if not any of those things, then maybe something more scientific, maybe they did nuclear testing here or something like that. I've read in books just how detrimental radiation poisoning can be."

"You're right, we need to find out everything we can about this beach, and the Boardwalk," Mark said.

Sam and I exchanged a look. This was insane.

The guys were talking like we were involved in some kind of crazy movie.

Mark and Shawn continued to hash out ideas as we all sat on the beach; they soon became engrossed in their conversation, throwing out one crazy harebrained idea after another.

While the guys hashed out ideas that could have been an episode of X-Files, Sam and I drifted away a little, so we could share some girl talk more openly.

"This is hard to believe," I said, still trying to wrap my brain around the ideas Shawn had thrown out. I sifted sand through my hand and watched as it cascaded through my fingers.

"I don't know. I'm kind of relieved that we're starting to figure things out. I would rather it be something crazy, than never knowing what happened. I hate not knowing where we're from or where our parents are," Sam said.

I felt a small wave of guilt for forgetting that Sam had always been by herself. Of course she would want answers. She had not been as lucky as me. I was loved and raised by two caring people.

"I'm sorry. You're right. Even if it's crazy, we still need to find out the truth."

I decided to change the subject. "So, what does Shawn think about this whole situation?" I asked.

"Well, like all of us, he wants to get to the bottom of all this, but I think he feels similar to me and just wants to find out what happened to his real parents. He had it pretty tough growing up too, but puts on an 'I don't care' attitude, so no one can see just how much it influenced him. His foster dad died five years ago, and Shawn hit the road. He said his foster dad was mean as a snake, and he wasn't taking the chance of being placed in another abusive foster home."

Our conversation was interrupted by the guys.

"Shawn and I think it's imperative that we start aggressively searching the internet to find out exactly what happened on this beach to tie all of us together."

"We don't have to leave right away though if you girls still want to ride more rides," Shawn added.

Though we were anxious to explore the internet to find out some answers, we voted, and decided it could wait a while. Sam still wanted to ride some of the rides at the Boardwalk. It was decided that we would play for a few hours and then get down to work.

I couldn't help my nagging feeling, like we were wasting time, but they had a point, the internet would be there later.

Sam lightened the mood as she dragged us on all the rides. I tried to balk when Sam headed back toward the "Giant Dipper," but she talked me into it.

The second time on the ride seemed to be faster than the first, and I my legs were quaking from the adrenaline rush by the time the ride screeched to a halt.

Mark laughed at my shaky legs when I tried to stand. He put his arm around me, to steady me. I took advantage of having him so close and snuggled in even closer. He didn't seem to mind; in fact he tightened his hold on me. As we made our way toward the exit of the ride, Sam started clamoring to ride the "Double Shot." The same ride mom and I had made fun of. It was hard to believe that just last week we had mocked the ride, and how lonely I had felt. Now, I was surrounded by people that felt like family, and that I could trust.

"No way," I said as Sam turned, pleading eyes on me.

"I think she needs to sit this one out Sam," Mark said.

Sam looked at my slightly green face and must have agreed with him, because they headed off by themselves to give the giant rubber band like ride a try.

Mark led me to a bench and sat down next to me. I laid my head on his shoulder and looked down at our linked fingers. Though his was much larger, our hands fit together as snuggly as a puzzle piece in the right slot. Usually, public forms of

135

affection mortified me, but I just couldn't seem to find a problem with this.

"I love you," Mark said quietly.

"What?" I said, still wrapped up in what his touch was doing to me.

"I love you," he repeated a little louder this time. "I know it may be too soon to say it, but I needed you to know how I felt."

I sat in silence for a few moments.

"I'm not trying to rush you," Mark said, sounding slightly panicked.

"It's not what you said. It's just, are you sure? I know we've shared the dreams all these years, but aren't you slightly disappointed at how I turned out?" I asked, feeling my cheeks blaze up in embarrassment.

Mark laughed. "Are you kidding me? You're everything I imagined and more. I feel like the luckiest guy in the world."

"Are you sure? Even with all my flaws?" I persisted, pointing to my red cheeks to prove my point.

Mark ran his hand down my cheek. "I love everything about you; your smile, your quirky sense of humor, but most of all your sensitivity. We are a match."

Love. He had said the word that I craved to hear the most. Sure, I heard it growing up, but I always felt my adoptive parents had to say the words. I knew that not all people loved me, case in point, my own real parents obviously had not. To think that just this morning, I had been tempted to throw in the towel when I thought he might leave me, but instead he was professing his love for me.

"I love you too."

Sam and Shawn joined us before we could say anything else. Sam's cheeks were flushed from the excitement of the ride, or maybe it was from being with the guy she was in love with.

Sam was able to talk me into going on the "Haunted Castle," which was just cheesy enough that all of us were laughing when we got off the ride.

We ended our day at the Boardwalk by going on "Loggers Revenge," which was a ride where you sat in a wooden log drifting along on the water until finally you drop off a hundred foot decline splashing at the bottom, so the water completely drenches everyone on board.

I put an end to the rides after that. I felt like I had left my stomach at the top of that drop, and now that I was soaked, I was ready to leave.

We decided that it would be best to do our research on the internet at Mark's house, since I still hadn't told my mom about Mark.

Sam and I called our mom's to tell them we were going to the movies, and out to eat afterwards.

I felt terrible about lying to my mom yet again. I was not the type of person who lied and the guilt was eating through me until Mark hugged me. I marveled at the warmth that spread through me at his touch. All the guilt seemed to flow away to make room for his warmth.

137

"Thanks," I said, he knew instantly what I was talking about. "I figured out yesterday that we neutralize each other's abnormalities. When I was angry at Matt yesterday, you touched my face and it was like a blanket being thrown over a fire," he told me.

Shawn and Sam were listening to our conversation, but didn't look surprised.

"We figured out the same thing when we first got together. It's almost like we were put together to even the other person out. I've discovered that when I'm at school away from him, I am almost in physical pain. This week has been especially tough because I've been with you all week, but at least the dreams seem to replenish us during the night." Sam said, looking at me.

I felt terrible. "Sam, you should have something. I wouldn't have been so selfish with your time."

"Get out of here. Shawn and I knew it was important that I spend time with you, once I realized that we shared all these crazy traits. Yeah, it has been tough, but in the long run, it's more important that we figure out all this insanity. Besides, I like hanging out with you," she said, reaching over to give me a quick hug. Her warmth wasn't as strong as Mark's, but it instantly began to sooth me.

We all piled into Mark's charcoal Navigator.

"Nice car man," Shawn said, running his hand over the smooth leather.

"Yeah it's nice," Mark said in an offhand manner, using a tone I didn't recognize. "Sorry, my dad used it as bribery for missing my graduation. He didn't even buy it; he had his assistant do it. I feel like a sellout every time I drive it, like I approve of his absentee parenting." Mark cut off his tirade as he pulled into a spectacular driveway.

Shawn let out a long whistle. "Wow dude, your dad must be loaded. This house is unbelievable."

It was every bit as beautiful as the houses I had admired on our drive to the beach the previous week.

"Thanks, I talked my dad into buying a house on the beach when we first moved here. I do admit, I did use the absentee father card on that one."

The house was breathtaking; it looked like it belonged on some swanky T.V show. The side that faced the road looked like it was constructed of driftwood you would find on the beach. The front doors were made from the richest oak I had ever seen. Each held a beautiful stain glass window that resembled the crashing waves of the ocean. Conch shells and miniature tiki lamps lined the sidewalk. The driveway was made up of thousands of crushed shells that crunched pleasantly underfoot. The lawn was lush with palm trees placed strategically around to give a person the feeling that they were on their own private little island.

Mark opened the front door and we all stopped in awe. The inside was even more breathtaking than the outside. The side of the house that faced the ocean was made up of glass panels from floor to ceiling that were only broken up by a set of oversized French doors leading to the patio outside. The plush carpet in the living room swallowed up our bare feet as we made our way toward the patio.

I walked over to the patio doors and opened them up. Inhaling the fragrant ocean air, I looked at the deck in wonder. Jeez, his dad must be loaded; I thought echoing Shawn's sentiments. The patio held one of the infinity swimming pools that I had only seen in movies. It seemed as if it was stretching out into the horizon. Lounge chairs were scattered abundantly across the patio and a wood patio table big enough for a party of twelve sat in the far corner next to the outdoor bar. The whole look was completed by a magnificent freestanding waterfall.

"Wow, is your dad a movie star or something?" Sam asked.

Mark laughed. "No, just a businessman."

Mark came over and stood by me. "This is beautiful," I told him.

"I know; I love it here. When we decided to move, my dad left the house hunting up to me and I fell in love with this one the moment I laid eyes on it. My dad travels so much, it feels like mine."

"Your dad must be good at his job to be able to afford this," I commented.

"He owns his own company, he's a troubleshooter. He goes in and helps companies that are having problems get back on their feet. He's earned quite a reputation and is in high demand. The only problem is that he's always out of town, working. I used to get upset about it, but then it just became normal."

Mark took my hand as we walked down the wooden steps that led to the beach.

"What a crazy day," I said as we removed our shoes.

"You're right about that. How are your emotions handling all of this?"

I was touched by his concern. "Their okay, I had a few iffy moments when Shawn was talking about all the UFO stuff, but I was able to pull myself together."

"Let me know if they become a problem, I want to help if I can."

I gnawed on my thumbnail as we walked toward the water edge. It would be tough to confide in him on that. I had spent my life trying to hide that aspect about myself.

The cool water lapped at our feet as we watched the sun begin to set on the horizon.

Mark cupped my shoulders as I slowly turned my face toward him. "There's something I have wanted to do all week, but I wanted to wait for the perfect moment," he said in a low voice as he stared into my eyes.

My heart began to beat heavily, and I lost myself in his warm brown eyes as his face began the decent toward mine. At the last possible moment, my eyes fluttered close. I was caught off guard at the rightness of it all. It was like walking in a meadow filled with flowers or sitting in front of a fireplace on a cold winter day. The warmth of the kiss took my breath away. I felt like I had finally come home. Mark tightened his arms around me, drawing me even closer.

The feelings that welled up in me were so tender, I felt like I could weep.

I was reminded of a conversation I had with my mom when I was thirteen. I had been observing the ease that my parents had around each other for weeks. They always seemed to know what the other needed. Often, I would observe them acting like they had just fallen in love. I asked my mom why that was. She told me that the love she felt for my dad at that moment was different than the love she had felt for him in the beginning. It was stronger and much more intense. "He's not only the man I love, but also my best friend. I love your dad more today than I ever have. Our love has evolved into something else because of the way we respect and listen to each other's needs," she had said.

That was how I felt in Mark's arms. This kiss may be our first, but it felt like I had kissed him a thousand times before.

I now knew my place in the world. It was by his side. We may have just met, but we had known each other our entire lives.

When we drew apart he said, "Wow."

I knew exactly what he was talking about; it had been a "Wow" kind of kiss.

"Let's try that one more time," he said, pulling me close again.

This time, I had my eyes closed before our lips met. The air around us seemed to sing. I lost myself in the kiss. My heart was racing and my skin tingled on every surface of my body.

"That was amazing," Mark said when our lips parted.

I would have spoken, but my head was still spinning.

"We better join the others," he said, grabbing my hand as we walked back toward the staircase.

I put my shoes back on, feeling dizzy in a drunken haze. If I knew kissing him was going to be that mind blowing, I would have forced myself on him the first day. He was right to wait though; the moment couldn't have been more perfect. I knew I would never forget our first kiss, the way his lips had felt, the way my heart had raced, and the way the cool ocean water lapped at our feet.

We stopped on the top step when we saw Shawn and Sam sharing the same kind of intense kiss that we ourselves had just experienced.

"Should I get the hose?" Mark asked with a laugh.

They sprang apart, both looking dazed as Mark and I laughed.

Walking into the living room, we all settled on the oversized pillows that were littered around on the plush cream colored carpet.

Mark used a remote to turn the Bose stereo on, and soon music was playing from the many speakers around the room.

He turned on his laptop and booted up the internet.

We started our search by simply Googling, 'Santa Cruz.' The sites that popped up were typical. Town history, chamber of commerce, and other sites that would help you find more information on the inner workings of a city.

Mark clicked out of that page, and changed the search.

"Strange occurrences in Santa Cruz," I read over his shoulder.

Mark shrugged his shoulders. "I figure we have to start somewhere."

From this inquiry, all kinds of weird sites popped up, as the internet tried to match up the request.

Mark used the mouse to scroll down the page as we all looked for something to jump out at us.

Some of the things that popped up boarded on downright kooky. The beach was popular with leftover die hard hippies and their laid back attitudes and open use of drugs, which had caused some problems in the early eighties. Besides that, the most frequent item that popped up were the countless shark attacks over the years.

After a while, I stood up to ease my sore backside from sitting on the floor so long. Walking around the living room, I studied the formal shots of Mark as he progressed through childhood. Even as an adolescent, he had been handsome. I stopped in front of his high school graduation picture and smiled at his boyish grin as he held up his diploma.

"He looks so young in that picture," Sam commented as she picked up the picture.

"He was, barely fifteen. I couldn't have imagined facing college that young. I'm intimidated thinking about it next year and I'm three years older than he was."

"I'm starved," Shawn said behind me breaking into our conversation.

"Me too, there's a great Mexican restaurant up the road I always go to. You guys want to give it a try?"

"I'm in," Sam said, setting the picture back down.

Mark looked at me. "So am I, I love Mexican food."

Chapter 9

Mark took us to a small family owned Mexican restaurant that was about a mile up the road from his house.

The parking lot was full and Mark circled the building before he pulled into a tight space between two oversized SUV's.

When we walked through the doors, I felt like we had crossed the border into Mexico. The walls were covered in authentic woven blankets and the brightly colored Piñatas that ran along the rafters gave the restaurant just the right amount of festiveness. A live mariachi band walked around the room encouraging everyone in the restaurant to join in the singing, it was a great atmosphere.

Sam was practically humming as she surveyed the great deco, excitedly pointing out one unique piñata after the next. Shawn looked down at her obviously enthralled by her exuberant attitude.

"Hey Mark," the man behind the counter greeted us. "Give me a few minutes and I'll get a table cleared off for you."

"That's fine, Miguel. Thanks."

"I love this place," Sam said as Shawn slung his arm around her shoulders. She pointed to another piñata that was fashioned like a giant maraca. "I love that one."

Five minutes later, the hostess guided us to our table.

"Nice to see you again Mark," said the pretty waitress as she passed our table.

"I eat here a lot," Mark explained as I raised my eyebrows at him.

The same pretty waitress came back to our table and set an overflowing basket of warm tortilla chips and salsa on the table. "What can I get you guys to drink?" she asked with eyes on Mark alone as she popped her gum in the process.

"Cokes for everyone?" Mark said, looking at all of us for confirmation.

"Sure honey," she said in a nauseating sweet voice.

Sam stifled a laugh, looking at me as the waitress sashayed away.

Shawn burst out laughing at Sam's attempt to mimic her by fluttering her eyes at Mark.

To reassure me, Mark slung his arm around my shoulders and pulled me close.

"Do you really think I have ever looked at another girl?" He whispered into my ear.

I shook my head, nervously working on the already low thumbnail on my right hand. I had never looked at another guy, and I knew he was the same, but knowing that didn't help the small flash of jealousy that shot through me when she smiled at him like he was some kind of delectable dessert or something.

Mark gently pulled my hand away from my nervous gnawing.

"It's always been you, nobody else," he continued.

"I know, I just don't like other girls to look at you. I know that seems possessive, but I can't help it," I tried to explain.

"Believe me I know. I've experienced it all week when I've watched the guys at school check you out when you walk by," he said as I shook my head in denial.

With all the California blonde bombshells walking through the halls of school, I was pretty sure the male population of the school was too busy checking them out. The girls at school weren't afraid to show off their long tan legs, and expose enough cleavage to keep the guy's eyes glued on them.

"They watch you because not only are you pretty, but you also walk around all aloof, so you pose a challenge for all the young studs of the school. They can get the other girls any old time, but you have enough of a mysterious air about you to snag all of their attention. That's the only reason Matt's giving us a hard time right now, he doesn't like the fact that you snubbed him."

I didn't agree with him. I personally felt that Matt was harassing us because that's what Matt did. He liked to torment those around him. Mark thought I was pretty because I had been in his dreams all these years. If not for that, he would see just how ordinary I was. Not that I ever wanted him to think of me like that, it was flattering for him to call me beautiful.

148

The waitress came back to our table to take our dinner orders. While we were waiting for our food, we discussed the issue that was the most pressing.

The idea that there could be four more people out there that may also share our connection was a twist none of us had ever considered.

We stopped talking when our food arrived. Mark was right, the food was excellent. I was famished, lunch had been hours ago. As we ate, our conversation became more light hearted as Shawn kept us laughing with stories about things that go on at the Boardwalk. He was a great story teller and we soon had a good grasp on the kind of people he worked with.

"They are definitely different than us," he said with a smile.

After dinner, we headed back to Mark's house to resume our conversation. I settled myself on one the comfy couches, tucking my legs up under me. Mark sat down next to me which of course sent my heart off its normal rhythm. Sam and Shawn took the other couch and Shawn tucked Sam up against his side.

"Well, I'm not sure what the picture means," I said, opening up the conversation. "But, I don't know if I buy all of your theories. They all just seem too kooky for me, this is real life not some fantasy book," I said, looking at Shawn.

"How do you know? Maybe this connection is from some kind of radioactivity coming from another planet," Shawn said as we all burst out laughing. "Hey, I've read lots of sci-fi and that's always what it boils down to. Some alien life form or something like that," he tried to explain as we continued to laugh.

"I'm not sure that's the reason for the connection, but Shawn is right, even the ridiculous things need to be examined. People just don't walk around feeling some odd connection with others, and they don't have dreams every night about the same person. We need to explore everything, look into things that could have created this link between all of us. We also need to consider the fact that there are four others out there that could potentially be just like us," Mark said, sobering up the lighthearted atmosphere.

He was right, as much as we would like to be normal teenagers, the plain and simple fact was, there was nothing normal about us. We had never been normal though we may have tried to pretend to be, but there was no denying our abnormalities.

"You know what I've been thinking?" Sam finally said.

"What?"

"Well, if there are only four couples in this picture, but eight children all together in the picture, it stands to reason that some of us must be related."

Mark and Shawn looked up from the computer at Sam's words. Neither seemed shocked at the suggestion, but I was reeling from the idea.

"You mean you think Mark and I are related?" I said, horror ringing through my words.

Mark took my hand trying to calm me. "Not us," he said with a slight smile in his voice. "Shawn and I think that maybe you and he are brother and sister."

"That would explain why you look so much like Shawn," Mark told me.

Brother and sister? Shawn and I were siblings? All my life, I had often wondered if I had any other family members, and here I was possibly sitting with my brother. I glanced at Mark, he didn't look surprised, and neither did Shawn.

"We suspected it as soon as I saw you standing next to Shawn when Sam introduced him to you. It's hard to deny your resemblance to each other," Mark said.

He paused.

"Is there more?" I asked.

"Well, we speculated that maybe Sam and I are related also, but we discarded it right off the bat. First, our builds are completely off, with her being a 'shrimp' and all. Plus, our skin tones don't match. Which means that possibly, one of the other kids in the picture might be my sister," he added. "Sam's brother could be one of the other boys in the picture," he continued.

I looked over at Sam's face and could tell from her intrigued expression that she was as curious as me. "A brother," she said in a weepy voice. The idea gave me a lump in my throat that matched the look on Sam's face. It was obvious she was as shocked as me.

Shawn instantly got up and put his arms around her to comfort her.

"I'm sorry," Sam said. "I'm trying not to cry."

Shawn picked her up and placed her on his lap, rocking back and forth rubbing her back as he showered light kisses on her face.

The emotional connection between Sam and Shawn was obvious. He was immediately able to calm her down and neutralize her emotions.

Watching Sam's reaction to the news hit me in a profound way. I never felt the wave of confusion come. It came out of nowhere and knocked the air right out of me. I had been struggling all night to keep my emotions in check, but this newest development in our conversation had finally triggered it and the emotions finally won.

Instead of turning to Mark for his strength and healing touch, I did what I always have done. I closed myself off from everyone else and bolted toward the bathroom. The sickness hit me wave after wave and I threw up wretchedly in the toilet. Finally, the waves subsided and I rested my head weakly on my hand.

I felt a cool rag being placed on the back of my neck.

"Has it passed?" Mark asked, in a concerned voice.

"You have to touch her Mark. It will speed up her recovery." I could hear Sam tell him, but her voice sounded far off as the pounding in my ears drowned everything else out.

"I'm fine. I'll be out in a moment," I said, hoping he would just leave. If my body hadn't just been overrun by emotions, I would have been embarrassed.

Mark ignored the hint and reached out to rub my back. I instinctively shied away from his touch, embarrassed to have him so close when I had just puked up an entire days worth of food. He insistently leaned in even closer, and I could feel the heat radiating out of him. An electric current seemed to flow through us, and I could feel the sickness beginning to ebb away. I kept my eyes closed as his touch soothed the rest of the sickness away. I finally let all my inhibitions fade and I leaned back against him, using his body heat to try to contain the chills that began to creep over my body.

Mark felt my sudden quaking and scooped me in his strong arms. I kept my eyes closed as he walked down the hall. He laid me on a bed and pulled a blanket up around me. After he had the blanket tucked firmly around me, he crawled on the bed beside me and pulled me snuggly in his arms.

We lay there quietly for a while as his soothing presence slowly began to help my weak body recover from the sickness. It seemed to take longer than normal because I had dealt with so many emotions in one short week, but finally, the chills receded and my mind began to drift as my body begged for rest.

"Before you go to sleep, you need to call your mom."

He was right. I got so comfortable lying there in his arms, I'd forgotten all about my mom. I started to sit up, but Mark pushed me lightly back down.

"I'll go get your cell phone."

He was back within a few moments and handed me my phone. I dialed my mom's cell number and waited for her to pick it up.

"Hey honey," she said as soon as she answered.

"Hey Mom, Sam and I had such a good time tonight, and Sam asked if I wanted to stay over," I said, trying to inject enthusiasm into my voice.

"That's fine," she said, sounding thrilled. I knew she was ecstatic that I had finally made a friend.

"I'll call you in the morning."

"That's fine, have fun."

I hung up the phone. I should have felt guilty for lying to my mom twice in one day, but the bout of sickness prevented any other emotions.

I closed my eyes as Mark continued to hold me in his arms. My mind drifted and I sunk into a deep sleep.

My sobbing woke us both up. I felt him wrap his arms around me.

"I'm here," he said. "I'm never going to leave you," he murmured in my ear.

The sobs subsided at his soothing words. He was here with me. I loved him so much, and it was so hard to be ripped away from him every night. He continued to whisper in my ear, telling me how much I meant to him and soon the dream faded away.

"Do you feel better?" he asked.

I thought about it for a moment, and surprisingly, I did feel better. I felt grimy from the sickness that gripped me last night, but besides that I felt much better.

"I think I would like to take a shower, but besides that, I feel much better. I'm so sorry you had to see that again. Would you believe, I've never had this many episodes in one week? Well, except when my dad died."

"That's what worries me," he told me. "Sam says it's not good for you to be having so many episodes."

He brought up something I had been wondering about.

"Why isn't Sam having these attacks?" I asked him.

"We talked about it while you were sleeping. Sam thinks it's because of the rough childhood she had; that she is able to control it better. Plus, she thinks that a lot of this is fear, and she dealt with fear enough when she was growing up, so it doesn't affect her as badly; not to mention the most important thing, which is letting Shawn sooth her." He said chidingly.

"I know. It's just a little tough for me to let someone in. I've spent my life handling all of this on my own."

"Come on, I'll get you some clean towels so you can take a shower," he said, changing the subject as he helped me to my feet.

He left me at the bathroom with clean towels and a new toothbrush. I turned on the water. While I waited for it to heat up, I looked in the mirror, cringing when I saw my reflection.

"Oh my gosh, I look terrible," I moaned.

My eyes were swollen from the tears and my skin was pasty from throwing up so much. Every hair on my head

155

seemed to be sticking up in every direction from sleeping on it. I resembled a scarecrow in a corn field. I could not believe I let him see me looking this bad.

I stepped into the spacious shower and let the water wash over me, wiping away the last traces of the sickness. I stayed in the shower for a long time, gathering my thoughts and finally, filing some of the information away.

I finally turned off the water and dried off. Mark had given me a pair of sweats and a sweatshirt; I pulled them on, dropping the towel at my feet. They were baggy, but I didn't care, they smelt just like him. I inhaled deeply enjoying his scent.

After I brushed my teeth, I left the bathroom and went off to search for Mark. I found him in the kitchen; he was finishing up fixing two cups of hot chocolate.

"I thought you might want a pick me up," he said as he handed me one of the steaming mugs. "I thought we could take these out to the patio while the others sleep."

Now that he mentioned it. Where were Sam and Shawn and where were they sleeping?

As if he could read my mind, Mark smiled. "Sam's crashed in my dad's room and Shawn took my room," he said.

I felt relived. I knew that Sam was her own person, but for some reason I felt responsible for her. I knew I was being a hypocrite. Hadn't I slept in the arms of the love of my life? Sure, I had been sick, but still.

We headed out to the patio. It was only 4:00 a.m., but the temperature outside was nice and mild. Mark helped me settle onto one of the patio chairs.

I took a sip of my hot chocolate. "That's good," I said as the hot chocolate ran down my throat.

"I added extra chocolate," he said with a smile.

I returned his smile as I took another drink of the rich concoction. I could definitely get used to this. This is how it will be if we ever married, I thought wistfully to myself as a whole new warmth spread throughout my body.

"It's so nice out here," I said, sighing.

"I know what you mean, there's nothing like the sounds of the ocean. Especially at night, the ocean seems to have a mysterious feel about it."

Mark reached over and grabbed my hand. I studied his warm masculine hand in mine. I cringed when I saw his nice even fingernails next to my own ragged ones. My nails looked pitiful in contrast. I really need to stop chewing on mine, I couldn't help thinking.

Shawn and Sam joined us on the patio shortly after dawn.

Mark and I had spent the last two hours talking about anything and everything. Mark asked me about college and I told him my plans to go to school locally.

I told him about my aspirations to help others, how I hoped to major in human relations in college.

"I want to be there for those in need. I would like nothing better than to set up foundations that would help others. It doesn't matter if it's as simple as raising money for books that volunteers could read to children in the hospital, or as big as finding funding to open a soup kitchen for the homeless. I just want to help," I said empathetically.

"That's what I love about you. You put the needs of others ahead of yours. I've watched as you struggled with guilt from lying to your mom and putting her peace of mind ahead of yours. I feel so lucky that the woman of my dreams turned out to be so fantastic."

After two hours of talking, all remains of the dream had vanished. By the time Sam and Shawn found us, I felt at peace.

"Are you feeling better?" were the first words out of Sam's mouth as she perched at the bottom of my lounge chair.

"Yes much better," I said, drawing my knees up so she would have more room to sit.

"You have to try to control it better. It's not good for your body to keep going through this. I'm going to try to show you some tricks that I picked up while I was growing up that seemed to help me cope. I want you to practice them and learn to use them. I'm worried that you're endangering yourself and I don't want you to wind up in the hospital. We love you and need you," she said giving me a quick hug. "You need to trust Mark more, let him know when the emotions are going to attack." She whispered in my ear.

I was touched by Sam's speech. I knew I could always count on my parents growing up, but I had always felt like the odd man out around other people. My childhood was lonely, friendless, and now for the first time, I was surrounded by three people who made me feel like I belonged.

158

"Well, I don't know about the rest of you, but I'm hungry, and unless all of you feel like eating left over take-out Chinese food from who knows when, we will have to go out for breakfast."

"Well, as much as I would like a good case of food poising from old take-out, I opt to go out to breakfast," Sam piped in.

"Me too, I'm done with throwing up for a while, let's head out," I said.

I waited as the others got ready to go. I already changed back into my clothes from the day before. Mark had thrown them into the wash while we were talking.

I needed to pick my mom's car up from the Boardwalk and take it home. All of us would have liked to stay together another night, but tomorrow was a school day, and I knew, there was no way my mom would let me stay at "Sam's" on a school night.

Sam did think it would be easy for her to talk her foster parents into letting her stay over at my house since they would be busy in court all week. The trial for their case was finally starting, and the time they weren't in court would be spent at the office preparing for the next day.

I felt I could play on my mother's sympathies to let Sam stay over.

We swung by Sam's on the way to breakfast so she could pack an overnight bag. I told her to pack extra just in case we were able to con extra nights from my mom.

I knew if I had to be separated from Mark, I at least wanted Sam to be with me.

The Boardwalk was packed when we finally showed up, stuffed from breakfast, to pick up my mom's Focus. I groaned when I saw the parking ticket sticking out from under the windshield wiper. "Great, how will I explain this to my mom?"

I got out of Mark's car and walked to the front of my mother's car. I pulled the ticket out from under the wiper blade and looked at it in dismay.

"Seventy-five bucks!" I screeched. "You have got to be kidding me!"

Mark came over and grabbed the ticket from me. He folded it up and put it in his pocket.

"You don't have to do that," I said, embarrassed that I made such a big deal about it.

Mark watched as color began to stain my cheeks. He leaned forward and gave me a kiss. I forgot my train of thought as I lost myself in his kiss. I liked that he was a neutralizer for me; the kisses were a definite bonus.

"We're going to work on those tricks later;" I heard Sam mutter behind me. "He's not going to be there every time."

I heard her muttering more, but I tuned her out as I kissed Mark one last time. It would be almost twenty-four hours until I saw him again, and my heart already ached, thinking about the separation.

I noticed that Sam was being unusually quiet.

I turned around to see her locked in Shawn's arms. I felt a twinge of guilt. Poor Sam and Shawn, they would be separated for longer than Mark and I. At least I would get to see Mark at school tomorrow. Sam would have to wait until after school to see Shawn again.

Mark and I stepped away to give them a few more minutes of privacy.

"You don't have to pay the ticket. It was my responsibility," I told Mark, making a grab for the ticket.

"I want to, anyway, Shawn and I planned on coming back to get it last night, but we forgot. Besides, I'm a working man and you're just a mere student," he said teasingly.

"Mere student," I said in mock anger. "You're a dirty old intern who preys on sweet innocent students," I teased.

"I like to prey on you," he said, raising his eyebrows suggestively.

He was joking, but my heart still skipped a beat. The idea seemed a little too appealing.

Sam and Shawn finally separated, and both looked quite flustered. Both had the same dazed look on their faces, like they had forgotten where they were.

We got in my mom's Focus.

Mark came over to the driver's side window to give me one last kiss.

"One to sleep on," he teased. "I'll call you tonight."

I had no trouble convincing my mom to let Sam stay over. I went for broke and pitched for the whole week. Playing on the fact that Sam's foster parents would be working late hours all week, and that Sam hated being alone at night.

My mom said it would be fine, but we had to promise to go to bed at a decent time.

"Just because you're in your last nine weeks of high school, I don't want you to fall off now."

I looked at her with humor. Was she forgetting that school was easy for me? Did she forget all those times everyone had commented on my IQ?

She saw my look and laughed. "Okay maybe not you, but school may not be as easy for Sam, so she needs to get enough rest."

Sam and I had of course kept it to ourselves that Sam's IQ was probably just as high as my own.

We both thought my mom's concern was funny.

Once we were in my room, Sam called her foster mom to ask her permission for the entire week at my house. Her foster mom was thrilled.

Sam told me after she hung up, that her foster mom admitted that they had been worried about leaving her by herself so much during the coming week.

We decided to continue surfing the web while we listened to some music.

I ran downstairs to grab a couple of sodas and a snack for both of us.

We ate our snack while we waited for my computer to boot up. Once the computer was ready, I typed in the words, "Strange links between people."Almost at once, a ton of options popped up. My eyes scrolled down the list and I was surprised to see a lot of sites on twins listed. I clicked on a random site and was amazed as I began to read.

"Listen to this," I said. "Twins that have been separated at birth will often suffer similar injuries in the same location on their bodies. They have also been found to marry similar spouses from the same backgrounds," I read on. "This paragraph says that twins often talk about the connections they share. It says it doesn't matter if they are identical twins or fraternal twins."

"I know none of us are twins, but we seem to share many of the same traits as twins," Sam mused.

I patted Feline absently on the head as he settled onto my lap. He was mad at me for abandoning him the night before, but couldn't turn down the attention. I stroked his fur as I continued to read more on twins.

"We share many similarities with the twins on this site, but their connection comes from genetics," Sam said as she read over my shoulder. "Well, except these ones." I said, clicking onto another site that had a more paranormal spin on it.

My first instinct was to laugh. "Give me a break. Some of these twins act like they're some kind of superhero," I said as I read how one twin was convinced that he and his brother were put on earth to save the world and that they could read each other's minds. "This is like reading the National Enquirer. I'm surprised he didn't add that his mother was an alien from another planet."

"Well, we mock it, but really Krista, is it any different than what all of us are going through? We dream about the same guy every night, we feel a surge of electricity when any of us touch, and not to mention; we all realized that we somehow freakishly neutralize each other."

She of course had a point.

We decided to call Mark to see if he and Shawn wanted to meet us at the park by my house.

Mark answered the phone on the first ring. "Sam and I stumbled onto something while we were searching the web," I said as a greeting.

"What kind of thing?" Mark asked, sounding intrigued.

"It's too much to explain over the phone. We were hoping you could meet us at the park."

"Sure we can. We're not doing anything except playing Xbox."

"Fifteen minutes too soon?" I asked.

"No, that's fine."

I hung up. "We better get ready; they're going to meet us there in fifteen minutes."

Five minutes later, we were heading down the stairs. "Mom, we're going for a walk," I yelled toward the back of the house. I heard a muffled reply and took it for an okay.

The day was pleasantly cool. I zipped my hoodie as we headed down the walkway. The small heat wave from the day before had lifted and there was a nice cool breeze rustling through our hair as we walked. We discussed the possibilities as to why we seemed to share so many similarities with sets of twins. Sam seemed to think that our moms might have been in some kind of test study. I was still pessimistic about the entire thing and didn't know which way to cast my vote. Both were crazy. I mean really, paranormal vs. sci-fi? I probably would have believed that I was a werewolf or a vampire easier than I seemed to be grasping this. At least that would be a lot cooler.

The guys were waiting at our usual picnic table at the park when we got there. We had only been apart for a few hours, but an ache I wasn't even aware of slowly began to dissipate. Every time I was away from him, I felt broken and incomplete, until we were reunited, then I felt whole again.

Chapter 10

I gave Mark a quick kiss, joining him on the top of the picnic table. I smiled as the familiar warm feeling began to spread through me. His kisses were becoming like a drug to me. They had a way of reminding me of all of my favorite things.

I pulled back to see him studying me intently. I felt a little self conscious as he continued to look at me.

I looked down to make sure I had nothing on my shirt.

I didn't see anything.

I rubbed my hand down my face, pausing at the corner of my lips to make sure I didn't have leftover food in the corners.

"What's the matter?" I asked.

"Nothing, I'm just amazed at how right life feels when you are with me. When we're apart, I try to fill the hole your absence leaves, but when I see you again, I feel complete."

I smiled at his words. They mimicked my exact thoughts. We were a cliché. We completed each other.

Mark smiled as if he had reached the same conclusion as me.

"So what did you two find out?" Mark asked, changing the subject.

I looked at him in confusion and then realized that he meant on the internet. His switching of gears threw me off track.

"Um, let's walk and we will fill you in."

Sam and I took turns filling them in on the things we learned about twins. We sparked their interest when we mentioned the many links that twins shared. I told them how I read one web site that suggested that some twins reported feeling the pain of their twin. Some even claim that they could read each other's thoughts.

"One woman even wrote that she had felt her sister's labor pains," Sam said.

"There was also one guy who said he knew when his twin brother died, even though he was nowhere near him," I added. "We know we're not twins, but we can't deny, we share similarities with them. There's other kooky stuff out there, but you guys would have to read it to believe it. I know it sounds farfetched, but it seems like the kind of stuff we've been searching for."

"You have a point; maybe we should start narrowing our search to scientific studies and anything paranormal we can find," Shawn said as we all digested the new information.

Sick of all the heavy talk, I headed toward the swings up ahead. I loved to swing. Not swinging up high of course; I just liked the feeling of swaying back and forth. I sat on one of the swings as Mark sat in the one beside me.

We linked hands while we watched Sam and Shawn's antics on the slide. Sam's laugh was contagious as she slid down the slide the first time. I couldn't help smiling just watching her.

Sam and Shawn looked carefree as they went from one piece of playground equipment to the next. They had a knack of being able to put the serious stuff aside and enjoying the moment. I envied their ease, I wished I could put the troubling thoughts on the backburner, but they were always there, butting in.

I watched as Sam and Shawn slid down the slide together, landing in a heap at the bottom, laughing as they landed in a tangle. Shawn pulled Sam close and kissed her.

I looked away feeling like an intruder. I turned to Mark and saw that he was watching me.

"Does it bother you that I'm not as carefree as they are?" I asked, indicating Sam and Shawn as they headed back down the slide.

Mark pulled the chains of my swing, twisting me around toward him. I looked intently into his eyes, waiting for his answer.

"I want you to listen to me. You seem to be under the misconception that there is something wrong with you, that there is nothing special about you. There is nobody else in the whole world that I would rather be with. I could look at you for hours and never get sick of it. I could spend every second of everyday in your presence and I would die a happy man. You belong with me," he finished as he gave the chains of my swing another tug, dragging me even closer as he kissed me.

I wound my hands around the chains of his swing and sighed as he deepened the kiss. I felt the warmth spread though me and wound my arms around his neck to pull him even closer.

I finally broke the kiss to find that I was sitting on his lap.

"How did I get here?" I asked as he laughed.

Mark changed the subject and brought up a point I had not thought of.

"So, I've been thinking, since the Dean knows about us, I don't see any reason why we need to keep our relationship a secret from your mom anymore," he said as we gently swung back in forth.

He was right; there really was no reason why we couldn't tell my mom about us. The fact that he was an intern at my school seemed trivial after all the things we had learned. He was so close to my own age, I didn't see my mom having a problem with us dating. I suspected it would be the exact opposite. She would probably be thrilled that I was seeing someone and not obsessing about my "dream" guy.

It would be nice to go out on an actual date with Mark. Plus, we could double with Sam and Shawn.

I smiled, things suddenly seemed so much better. The dark cloud that had been hovering over our heads moved away. We may not have found the answer to the turn our dreams have taken, but it no longer mattered, we had each other in reality and that was all that was important.

Sam and Shawn joined us and I glanced at my watch.

"We have enough time to walk around the park once." I said.

Our conversation was much more light- hearted, and Sam soon had us in stitches, making fun of the rich kids at our school. She gave the best imitation of the stuck up drama queens. "Oh my gosh! My nail polish doesn't match my shoes or watch. How will I ever face anyone again?" She said in a perfect imitation of one of the *Lush Trio*.

I had to hold my sides, I was laughing so hard.

It was nice to be around people who were on the same wave length as me. The more time I spent with Shawn, the more I liked him. I had put everyone's assumptions on the hold after my emotional melt down, but I couldn't help noticing small habits that we both shared. He rubbed his forehead a lot and I knew I did too. My dad used to tease me that I would rub a hole in my forehead if I didn't stop rubbing it. I also noticed that he laughed the same way that I did.

When I was in middle school, I tried to change my laugh to be more ladylike, but it didn't work. When I thought something was funny, it just seemed to burst out of me.

It was an unreal experience to see someone that shared many of my traits. Just watching him filled me with a sense of rightness.

"I hate to break up the mood, but we seem to have forgotten something important. What about the other four?" Shawn asked.

He was right; we had put the others out of our minds, but they could be ignored no longer.

"Hopefully, they're drawn to Santa Cruz also. If they are, then maybe we'll run into them. I know it's a long shot, but the four of us found each other, so it could happen," Mark said.

"I know how we can try to find them," Sam said. "We can search the internet for children that were abandoned around the dates we were abandoned. We now know their ages, so that should narrow the search down. Not to mention, that you need to talk to your dad," she said to Mark.

"I know," he said with a sigh. "My dad is so freaking straight laced though, that none of this seems like him at all. I've been trying to wrap my brain around the fact that he knows about all this since I saw Shawn's picture yesterday. I tried calling him on his cell phone, but of course it went right to voicemail. His secretary informed me that he's out of town for at least another three weeks or so, when I tried to call him this morning. She told me in an offhand way that he is way too busy to talk to me unless it's an emergency, but she would pass a message along to him," Mark said with sarcasm lacing his every word.

I reached out and grabbed his hand, hoping that whatever healing power we possessed would calm his anger and hurt.

"Well, until he gets back or calls you, we can do our own digging," Sam said.

Once we had a game plan, the guys decided they would walk us home. Now that we were going to tell my mom, I was anxious to introduce Mark to her.

It only took us ten minutes to walk back to my house.

I felt a serious case of butterflies in my stomach as we walked up my walkway.

I wasn't nervous; I just wanted my mom to think Mark was as great as I thought he was.

Mark grabbed my hand as we headed up the stairs of the front porch. Sam and Shawn opted to wait on the porch. They wanted to give us a little privacy as I introduced Mark to my mom.

My mom was on the couch watching a rerun episode of CSI. We were avid watchers of all the CSI shows.

She looked up when we walked in. Her smile of greeting turned to surprise when she saw that I was holding some strange guys hand.

I dragged Mark further into the living room as she stood up.

"Mom, I would like you to meet my friend, Mark. Mark, this is my mom, Cindy Miller.

My mom reached her hand out, Mark clasped it between his hands.

"I didn't know you made any friends other than Sam this past week?" She said, obviously fishing for more information.

I decided to go for broke. It was like pulling off a band-aid, quick and fast was the only way to go.

I plunged in.

"Mark's a year older than me," I started.

"A year older, how did you meet? Are you still in school?" She asked, posing the last question to Mark.

Mark looked over at me. I knew what he was asking with the look. I shook my head yes. We might as well get it over with.

"I go to Krista's school, but I'm not a student. I'm doing my graduate thesis at her school," he said.

I took over and filled in the rest of the blanks for her. I told her how he had skipped grades growing up, and was able to graduate from college last year. I told her how our love of history had given us a common bond and that we talked about it after school one day. Then I told her that Sam and I had run into him and his friend yesterday at the Boardwalk.

"Does the Dean know your dating a student?" she asked.

I thought I detected just a touch of accusation in her voice.

"Yes, and he was not happy about it," Mark said truthfully.

"Mrs. Miller, I know that it is unprofessional that I'm seeing your daughter. I have no excuse, except that I think she is pretty special, and I would like your permission to continue seeing her."

"I don't know if it's best for Krista to date an intern where she goes to school."

"Mom, we're going to keep it quiet, nobody will know except Sam," I said, starting to feel the first stirrings of doubt about telling her. What would I do if my mom wouldn't let me see him anymore?

"I don't think it's a good idea Krista. He's an adult. He goes to work every day while you're in school. You still have years of schooling ahead of you," she said.

"I'm sure you're a nice young man, but Krista's never even dated. I would prefer her first boyfriend to actually attend her school," she said to Mark.

"I was hoping you would feel differently," Mark said, looking disappointed.

I couldn't believe it. This was not the way it was supposed to go. My mom was supposed to be okay with it. She was supposed to be glad that I was finally interested in someone.

"Mom, I want to see him, I love him." The words slipped out. I wished I could take them back. I knew instantly that I had made a mistake, by the look on her face.

"Love him? You've only known him for a week, how can you love him?" She said angrily. "I don't want you to see each other again."

I was shocked.

Not see him.

My mom was crazy.

How could she think that we wouldn't see each other?

I became desperate. "Mom, he's the boy in my dreams," I blurted out.

"The boy of your dreams, what did you do, tell him about your dreams and he said he was the guy? Krista, it's a line. Of course he's going to tell you that he's the boy of your dreams."

I was in tears. "That's not true, he has the same dream as me," I said sobbing.

Mark made a move to comfort me, but my mom blocked him off.

"I think its best that you leave."

174

Mark tried to protest. "Mrs. Miller, if you would just give us a chance to explain. We'll tell you everything."

"I don't want to hear your explanations, you preyed on my daughter's sensitivity, and you exploited her dreams. *You need to leave!*"

I tried to protest through my tears, but it was too late. My stupid emotions had taken over. I rushed to the bathroom as my mom escorted the love of my life out the front door.

I was weaker than ever after my bout of sickness and was ashamed at the way my mom had treated Mark. I wasn't sure if I would ever be able to forgive her. I walked slowly to my bed and collapsed on it.

"Oh Krista, what happened?" Sam asked as she entered my room.

"She said we couldn't see each other," I said in a dead voice.

"Why?" Sam asked bewildered.

"Because, he's finished with high school."

"Krista, I know your upset, but we have to control it. I can't explain it, but I feel your body is getting weaker. You have to learn how to control it. I'm going to show you how."

"I don't want to learn," I said stubbornly.

I knew I sounded like a little kid who didn't get what they wanted. I was just so mad at my mom, and that my body had betrayed me yet again. I was weaker than ever, and I was sick of that.

Sam was having none of it. "I don't care if you don't want to learn. I'm not giving you the choice. Now sit up!" Sam said in a demanding voice that I never heard her use before.

With a resigned sigh, I sat up and looked at her.

"Okay, it's simple enough. You know how you briefly lose your breath when you kiss Mark? You need to copy that feeling. When your emotions start to get out of control you need to hold your breath and close your eyes. You need to deprive your emotions of the oxygen they feed on. It will go against what your instincts are telling you to do, because normally you suck air in when an attack begins. You need to train your body to do the opposite."

It sounded simple enough and even though I said I didn't want to learn how, I hadn't meant it. I was anxious to get my emotions under control. I was sick of them dictating my life.

I practiced for a few minutes with Sam, but then I had to lie back down. I was exhausted from the emotional upheaval that my body had gone through in the last twenty-four hours.

I apologized to Sam as I drifted off to sleep.

The dream woke me the usual way. I was able to stifle my sobs and Sam slept on.

I headed to the bathroom, closing the door softly behind me. I turned on the shower and stepped in. As the water cascaded over me, I thought about how I was going to convince my mom that Mark was the guy for me.

Last night it seemed impossible, but with the new day, I was ready to try again. It was bad enough that we were being separated in my dreams, but I was not going to let it happen in real life.

I sat in my sitting area reading while I waited for Sam to wake up. Once we were both ready for school, we headed downstairs for round two.

My mom was already up and fixing breakfast when we walked into the kitchen.

"Mom, can we talk about it?" I said in a pleading voice.

"There's nothing to talk about. I know you think he's you're dream guy, but he's just trying to manipulate you. You've never dated and your still naïve when it comes to guys."

I felt the anger and other emotions well up inside me. I tried Sam's trick and held her breath. Smother them back, I thought. It was much harder than I thought it would be and went against every instinct I had, but miraculously it began to work.

"You're wrong Mom, he loves me, and if you would just let us explain?" I said with a touch of anger in my voice.

"I don't want to hear explanations. I'm the adult. I know more about the things guys do to get a pretty girl. The subject's closed; you're not to see him again."

"Mom, he's in my history class, I'll see him in school. Please reconsider, you're being unreasonable," the pleading tone entered my voice again.

"Krista, I forbid you to see him; you're grounded. I will pick you up after school, and I want your cell phone before you go to school."

"What about Sam?"

I could not believe how she was acting. She'd never grounded me before. We had always gotten along. Why wouldn't she see reason?

"Sam can still stay over, we already told her foster parents. Sam you don't have to come home when I pick up Krista in the afternoons, but I would like you back at our house by at least six each night," my mom said, addressing Sam for the last part.

I felt the anger rise in me again. "You can't keep me away from him," I shot at her as I turned and walked out the door.

"Yes I can," I heard her mumble.

I waited for Sam on the front porch. I used Sam's method to fight back the waves of emotions. It was a little harder than it had been the first time.

I thought it was because a new emotion had emerged, despair.

Sam came over and gave me a hug and a look of sympathy.

"Don't worry, we'll figure this out and you will see him in a little while. We'll see what ideas the guys have. It's all going to work out."

"I'm proud of you for controlling the emotions," Sam added.

Sam's words cheered me up. She was right, in a few minutes we would be at school and I would see Mark there. I decided that I would go to his class before homeroom. I no longer cared about keeping our relationship a secret anymore; I just wanted to see him.

We walked briskly to school. Sam didn't protest the faster pace; she knew I was anxious to see Mark.

The front lawn was as crowded as ever and everyone was buzzing. I didn't give a second thought to what had gotten them all gossiping so early in the morning. They probably found out something shocking about another student and they were busy spreading it around.

Sam and I headed right to Mark's class.

I was disappointed to find his classroom empty. We decided to wait for him.

Sam chatted away about trivial things, trying to take my mind off the fight I had with my mom.

I appreciated her chatter; it quieted away the last lingering emotions. Despite everything that happened, I was proud of myself for fighting the emotions back, and I would be damned if I would let the emotions dictate my life ever again.

Mark was still not there as the first bell rang. His room began to fill up with his homeroom students.

"I heard he's in the office, something about a parent complaining," I heard a girl say to a friend as they walked in the room.

I looked at Sam. She shrugged her shoulders; neither of us knew what to think.

"Let's head to homeroom and we'll check back before first period since we'll be on this end of the building anyways," Sam said.

She was right. It would only make matters worse if my mom heard I was late to class.

We left the room and bumped into the last person I wanted to see.

"Looking for your boyfriend? I hear he's getting the ax. Seems some parent called complaining that an intern was dating her daughter," Matt said with an evil smile. "Could that be your mom, princess?" He added in a nasty tone.

He draped his arm across my shoulders. "Why don't you forget about good ol' teach and go out with me?" He said, trying to turn on the charm.

"I wouldn't go out with you if you were the last guy on earth." I said, jerking away from him.

His smile turned nasty again. "We'll see about that, you're going to get lonely without your boyfriend," he said as he walked away.

"My mom wouldn't do that. She wouldn't get a person fired from their job, no matter how angry she was," I said to Sam in a distressed voice.

"I think she would, and I think she did. You didn't see her face after you left the kitchen. She looked like a lioness protecting her cub. She thinks you're in danger, so she's protecting you."

"She can't do this. I can't be away from him," I said as the despair welled up in me. I felt the waves rolling in.

"I know, but you have to fight back the emotions," Sam said, from what sounded like a long way off. "Krista, you have to fight it.

I heard her in the distance, Sam was right. I needed to calm myself.

Everything felt like it was spinning. I held my breath and closed my eyes. "Go away," I thought as I fought to smother the waves.

Finally they receded. "I did it," I said, still a little shaky.

"Good job, I thought you were a goner there. I'm so proud of you. How do you feel?"

"Not bad, just a little weak, but I've had much worse," I said, looking at my watch. "We better hurry."

It seemed crazy to be rushing off to class when so much was going on. I couldn't wait until I was done with the whole school charade.

Sam and I slid into our chairs just as the bell rang. Neither of us missed how everyone went silent when we walked in the room. So, I was the new gossip material. "Twice in two weeks, that had to be a record," I thought, sarcastically.

The rest of the day passed at a snail's pace. Eventually, as the day progressed, the comments of the other students began to reach me. Surprisingly, the gossip didn't bother me. I had been the outsider so often, it no longer fazed me. All I cared about was what was going on with Mark. I was anxious to get to fifth period to see if he was there yet.

When the bell rang for fifth period, my heart began to race. When we walked through the classroom door though, my heart dropped like a stone.

He wasn't there. Only the teacher was there, and he was busy writing notes on the chalkboard. The rumors were true.

The class started to buzz.

181

They fired him, how could my mom do that to him? This was not the way she acted; usually, she was so even tempered and willing to talk things over. I felt betrayed. The rest of the class passed in a blur. I never opened my book and I didn't take a single note. I no longer cared.

The rest of the day passed much the same way. Every once in awhile, Sam would look at me with a look of sympathy mixed with worry. I appreciated her concern, but I could say nothing to reassure her. Though I learned to control the sickness, it didn't lessen the emotions that would try to race through me. By the end of the day, I was exhausted from fighting them back.

Feeling lethargic, I gathered my books. I missed Mark so much that my body ached, adding to the feeling of tiredness. Sam walked quietly by my side as we headed out the door.

I felt Sam's excitement as we exited the school.

I followed her eyes, Shawn was here. I scanned the area looking for Mark. My eyes filled with angry tears. He wasn't here. "Damn my mom for acting so irrational," I thought to myself.

Sam hurried to Shawn's side and threw herself in his arms. My heart ached and my insides seemed to clench inwards as I watched them.

Sam beckoned me over. "Shawn has a message from Mark."

"Mark said not to worry, he doesn't blame your mom she was just trying to protect you. He said that you two would find a solution. This works anyway because he and I are going to take a short road trip."

Sam was shocked. "You're leaving?" she asked anxiously.

He pulled her into his arms. "Only for a few days, we found out where one of the others was dropped off."

In my current dilemma, I had completely forgotten about the others. "Where?" I asked.

"New Mexico. We think it will only take three or four days for us to find out what happened to her."

"A girl?" I asked. "You found one of the cities where one of the girls had been left?" Even in my current frame of mind, I couldn't help feeling excited.

"Mark wants you to continue to practice with Sam and to be careful."

"Why, did you find something else?" Sam asked.

"No, we just want you to be safe while we're gone."

I had always been in tune with other people's emotions and could always sense when someone was lying. I could tell Shawn was hiding something. I looked at Sam and could tell she knew he was lying also.

I was just about to confront him when I heard a car horn beep. Everyone on the front lawn turned to look. Parents normally didn't honk.

"You have got to be kidding me," I muttered, "She is literally killing me."

Sam stifled a laugh.

"You have to go; Mark said he will call you later."

"He can't, my mom confiscated my phone," I said desperately.

"He'll call you on Sam's phone. I have to go now anyway, our plane leaves in a couple of hours, I love you," he said to Sam as he pulled her into his arms for one last kiss.

I walked away to give them a chance to say goodbye and climbed into the car without a word to my mom. Sam caught up to me and slid in the backseat beside me. My mom didn't question my silent treatment. Sam, feeling uncomfortable, was unusually silent.

After dinner, Shawn called Sam on her cell. I sat on my bed and let Sam use the sitting room so she could have a little privacy. After a while, she brought me the phone and quietly walked out of the room.

The moment I heard his voice, I began to cry. "It's going to be okay, we will work it out," Mark told me, trying to calm my tears.

"I know. I just miss you so much. I don't like being separated from you for twenty four minutes, let alone twenty four hours. My heart feels so empty with you gone," I told him.

"I know, it's the same for me. The separation is messing with me also. We've discovered it affects our bodies' quite strangely."

"What do you mean?" I asked him.

"I'll explain when I get home."

"I'm not going to let my mom keep us apart," I told him. "I can't handle the separation. Either she lets me see you, or I'm going to tell her I'm moving out. My birthday is in a few weeks and I will be eighteen."

"I don't want to cause friction between you and your mom."

"The friction is already there. I don't know if I will ever be able to forgive her for getting you fired. I love her and would miss her if it came down to that, but I can live without her. I don't think I could ever live without you."

"We'll work it out, try not to worry okay? Remember how much I love you."

We talked for a few more minutes and then said good night. He promised to call again the next day at the same time.

After the call, I was exhausted and fell right to sleep.

I woke up the next morning confused. I sat up and looked at Sam who was rubbing sleep out of her eyes.

Finally, Sam focused on my face.

"What's the matter?" She asked.

"He wasn't there last night, I didn't dream about the Boardwalk at all," I said panic stricken.

Sam looked alarmed. "You didn't dream about him?"

I shook my head no and lay back down. I felt light headed like I was sick or something.

"You look peaked, are your emotions getting out of hand?" Sam asked.

I shook my head no, it wasn't like that. I'd gone to bed with my heart aching from missing Mark, and awoke to find that the ache had spread throughout my whole body.

This wasn't emotional sickness, this was something else. Something I had never experienced before.

"Will you tell my mom that I'm too sick to go to school?" I asked Sam.

My mom came up to verify that I was truly sick. If I wasn't so sick, I would have dwelled on how much our relationship had changed over the course of thirty six hours.

My mom took one look at me and knew that I was sick. Sam wanted to stay with me, but my mom wouldn't let her skip school. Mom closed the blinds and turned off my bedroom lights after Sam left for school. I rolled over in a ball and sunk into an uneasy sleep.

Every few hours or so, my mom would creep in to check on me, and by the time Sam came home, she was as sick as me. It was obvious she had a case of what I had, or so my mom thought. We couldn't tell my mom that we were just suffering from separation sickness. She called Sam's foster parents and told them that Sam and I had picked up a bug. She assured them that Sam would be fine where she was. "I'm here anyway," I heard her say.

Sam and I dozed for the rest of the afternoon, and by the time the guys called, I didn't even have the energy to talk, I just wanted to sleep. Sam was feeling a little better than I was, so she talked to Shawn, but she kept it simple.

"I think you guys need to come home. We need you." Shawn didn't need any explanations, he told her that they found what they needed and would be on the first plane home in the morning.

Sam hung up the phone and told me. I heard her from far away. All I wanted to do was sleep.

I woke the next morning with my mom kneeling at my side.

"Honey you look so sick. I think I need to take you to the hospital."

"I just need Mark," I whispered as I drifted back to sleep.

I woke later to raised voices. Too weak to move, I laid there as the voices got louder. "You just have to trust me, but one way or another, I'm going in there."

I was too weak to even move as Shawn and Mark charged into the room. Shawn hurried to Sam's side and pulled her into his arms.

I could hear my mom trying to protest. My eyes drifted closed before Mark even reached my side.

I woke a few seconds later to Mark's hands on my face. I was in his arms and was finally able to open my eyes and keep them open.

"I don't think I can live without you," I said in a weak voice.

"I know that I can't live without you," he answered back.

He leaned over and kissed me. I felt the ache that was gripping my body begin to loosen its death grip on me. I deepened the kiss, and the familiar warmth spread though me. His touch was the nourishment I needed.

I could hear Sam and Shawn talking quietly. Sam had recovered quicker than me, probably because she hadn't been separated from Shawn as long.

Mark continued to rain light kisses across my face and soon I began to regain my strength. I could feel my heart began to find its normal rhythm again.

I was surprised when I finally looked up and saw my mom was still standing uncertainly in the doorway.

"We have to tell my mom something," I said in a whisper.

We could skim over the sketchier parts, but we had to give her something. I had wanted to keep her in the dark as much as I could and spare her all the details, but she had just witnessed my friend and I miraculously recover from a terrible illness by a few kisses from a couple of guys. She wasn't stupid and she would want answers.

Mark nodded his head.

"Mom, I know you're confused. We were too at first, but if you let us explain, you will start to understand," I said in a still weakened voice.

She nodded her consent, and the five of us headed down to the living room to talk. Sam and I were still weak, so the guys helped us down the stairs and got us settled on the couch.

My mom sat on one of the recliners in the living room and Mark perched on the edge of the other recliner. Shawn chose to lean against the wall.

I started from the beginning. I told her about having the dreams every night, not just every once in awhile, like I had led her to believe. I explained my first meeting with Mark, and the familiarity I felt the first time I met him. I then told her how he stepped out of the shadows of my dreams that first night. I explained that I feel like I had known him my whole life because he had always been in my dreams. I didn't mention any connections with Shawn and Sam except that they had similar dreams as ours. I knew there were numerous holes in my story, but I only wanted to give her the facts.

She listened quietly the whole time, and finally when I was done talking, she finally said something.

"You expect me to believe all that?" She asked incredulously.

"Come on mom think about it, do you have a better explanation for all of this?" "You saw how sick I was. Do you think I was faking that or what about all those times my emotions got out of control?" I said in a hurt voice.

"Of course not, it's just that all of this seems pretty farfetched; dreams about each other and getting sick because you were apart? How come you were fine away from him In Montana, but now you seem to have issues?"

"We don't know, Mrs. Miller. Believe me, we wish we did," Mark finally interjected.

"I don't like any of this," she said to him. "My daughter is only seventeen and you're already acting like she's yours."

"I realize we're young, but that doesn't seem to matter to the dreams. We just want to get to the bottom of those first. Everything else we can take slowly, one day at a time. I'm not trying to steal her from you," he said, finally zeroing in on what was really bothering my mom. She had just lost my dad less than a year ago, and now she thought she was on the verge of losing me.

I stood up and walked over to where she was sitting. Perching on the arm of the chair, I grabbed her hand. "Do you understand why I love him now? It's just like you and daddy. Remember when you told me you were more in love with him than the day you met, and each day your love grew stronger? It's the same way for us. We have been together forever. I love him because he is my past and my present, he is my life. These past few days were obviously a crucial test for us, and we now know that we can't live without each other. None of us know why, but that's what we're trying to figure out. I know this is crazy, but you know I've never been normal. You and dad did the best you could, but I was a nut job from the beginning," I said, trying to lighten the mood.

My mom looked from me to Mark. "I understand, but I don't know about everything else. This is a lot to accept, but I can't deny what he did for you this morning. You looked like you needed to be hospitalized."

"I guess I can't keep you apart. Just understand that I'm your mother. I just want you to be safe and happy," she said as she reached over and hugged me.

"I'll let you guys stay and talk for awhile. I'm going to go finish my painting," she said as she gave me one last quick hug.

"Mark, I'm sorry I called the school. I thought I was protecting Krista, it looks like I've lost that job," she said a little sadly as she headed out the door.

"Mom wait," I said, rising from my perch. "You will always be my mom and I will always need you. Just be happy that everything is going to work out," I whispered in her ear as I

190

gave her an out of the ordinary tight hug. I did not shy away from the emotions she was emitting; instead, I embraced them and cast them away. I was becoming quite proficient at fighting off the negative effects of mine and others emotions.

Sam and Shawn decided they were going to go for a walk when my mom retired to her art studio. Sam had most of her strength back and wanted some fresh air.

My recovery was a little slower. My body felt like it had been put through the ringer; the countless bouts of sickness this week had taken its toll. It was going to take me a little longer to recover.

Once we were by ourselves, Mark led me toward the couch and gently pulled me into his arms. He rained soft kisses along my jaw bone and up to my temple, leaving a heated trail where his lips had just been.

"I'm sorry you got so sick. I never imagined it would be like that if we were separated," he said in my ear, making shivers of delight race up my spine as his breath tickled my ear.

He chuckled at my response. "Ahh, so you like that?" He said in a husky voice that could only be described as the sexiest thing ever.

I nuzzled my face into his neck; it felt so good to be in his arms again. I felt bad that we had hurt my mom by telling her the truth, but it was worth it for this. I could stay in his arms forever.

I sat up suddenly, just remembering something that I had been meaning to ask him. "What did you mean the other night when you said that the separation was also affecting you?"

He chuckled slightly, a little embarrassed. "Once our plane landed, and we were so far away from you, we would get these small bursts of rage. They weren't directed at anyone, they would just come out of nowhere."

"Shawn broke the door of our hotel room when it wouldn't close right. He slammed it so hard that it split the wood down the door frame. I got mad for no reason and hit the rental car just before we left. It was hard to explain the dent to the rental company, but luckily I had bought the insurance for it. The rage didn't fully leave me until I kissed you in your room. The separations are getting harder and harder. Shawn and I talked about it, and we don't know why we could be separated all those years and not be affected. Yet now, we can't seem to make it more than twenty-four hours without each other."

I finally brought up what had been gnawing a hole through me over the past few days.

"The dreams have stopped," I said quietly

"I know. I didn't want to bring it up because I didn't want to upset you, but I've had it on my mind also. For the first time in my life, I'm not dreaming about the Boardwalk at all."

"Me either," I said sadly as tears flooded my eyes, "I miss it already."

Mark took my hand and lifted my chin so I could look in his eyes. He used his thumb to brush away a stray tear. "We may not have the dreams, but we have this," he said as he leaned down and pressed the sweetest kiss on my lips. I felt a rush of heat flow through me and I wrapped my arms tightly around his neck. For a moment, we were one. Our hearts took on the same rhythm and beat as one.

We broke apart when we heard a throat being cleared behind us. Flushing slightly, I turned to see my mom standing in the doorway.

"Oops! Sorry mom," I said.

"I was wondering if you could help me in the kitchen," she asked.

"Sure," I said, exchanging a look with Mark, she obviously wanted to talk to me alone. I sure hoped that she hadn't changed her mind about letting me see Mark.

I followed her though the swinging kitchen door. We stood there for a minute, awkwardly.

"Why don't we sit at the table for minute?" She eventually said.

The silence stretched in front of us.

"Mom, just say it," I said, getting antsy from the silence as I patted her hand.

She finally plunged in. "I know you have these strong feelings for him and he seems to share those feelings, but I hope you decide to take it slow before you go too..." she trailed off.

Oh no, she was giving me the *sex* talk. I didn't know whether to laugh or bury my head in embarrassment.

"I know you know about sex, but I don't know if you know how personal it is. How sacred it is the first time...."

"Mom, I know it's special, we're not going to rush into anything. We have been so busy trying to figure out our past, we haven't even made it to second base yet."

She raised her eyebrows. "Yet?" she asked.

I laughed. "Mom, I love him. Eventually, we're going to make it to second base, or I hope we do," I said, laughing again at the look on her face.

"I promise we will take it slow. Truthfully, I always imagined myself waiting for my wedding night. I know that sounds old fashioned, but I've always wanted to save it for that special day."

Relieved, she reached over and hugged me. "That sounds like a great idea."

"I'm sure it does," I said wryly.

She chuckled. "I'm your mom. You can't blame me for wanting you to wait."

I laughed with her, more out of relief that she was finally accepting Mark. I suddenly felt lighthearted. I hugged her for good measure and headed back to the living room. I found Mark lounging on the couch reading one of my favorite books. He set the book aside when I came back in the room.

"Everything okay?"

"Everything is fine. She gave me the sex talk," I whispered with humor.

"Oh!" Mark said, flushing slightly.

"What did you tell her?" he asked, pretending indifference.

"I told her it was too late. We had already done it," I said mischievously.

"What?" Mark said in shock, jumping to his feet.

"Got you!" I said giggling, while I backed away as he began to advance toward me.

"You think you're funny don't you?" He asked as he reached out and caught me. I giggled as he carried me back to the couch.

"You almost gave me a stroke. I didn't know if I should hit the door running in case your mom was coming after me with a shotgun."

I giggled again still tickled from the look he had on his face. "You should have seen the look on your face," I said between my merriment.

"You are so beautiful when you laugh, your whole face lights up, it makes me happy just to see it," he said as he stroked the side of my face with the back of his hand.

The laughter stuck in my throat as a new heat began to fill me. When he looked at me like that, I felt like the most special person in the world.

Chapter 11

Once Sam and Shawn came back from their walk, we decided to enjoy my newfound freedom and go out to dinner.

We picked a local pizza place downtown that Mark swore was the best around. Now that he was no longer working at my school, there was no reason we needed to avoid the restaurants around our school.

The pizza place was loud and crowded with students when we arrived. A hush seemed to fall on the place when we pushed through the doors. It ended quickly, as the gossip hounds turned away, trying to act like they weren't staring.

I spied Matt in a corner booth with a bunch of his cronies. Mark spotted him at the same time, I had to swallow a laugh when he pulled me close and planted a sensual kiss on my lips, leaving no question that we were together.

Sam snickered beside me. She knew exactly what Mark was doing. Shawn looked a little confused, so we filled him after we claimed a table in the back. He slapped Mark appreciatively on the back as they got up to place our order at the old fashioned counter with swivel stools.

"You look so much better," Sam said, studying me.

"I feel better, and now that I can do your breathing trick, I feel like I'm finally turning a corner."

"I'm glad. We all need to be in tip top shape. I can't shake the feeling that something bad is going to happen."

The guys came back and I was happy for their intrusion. I was sick of worrying about all the doom and gloom. I just wanted to bask in the moment like any other teenager. Soon, we were all laughing at more of Shawn's anecdotes and the conversation flowed lightly around our table. It was hard not to notice the envious stares directed at us from the gossip hounds, probably wondering how we had gotten so close and at ease with each other. Their conversations seemed superficial compared to the ones that our group was sharing.

The bell rang for our pizza and the guys went and grabbed it along with a pitcher of soda. The pizza was excellent. The cheese was melted a golden brown and oozed over the sides with each bite we took. I ate until I was filled to the brim. The guys ate us under the table; we teased them about how much pizza they had consumed.

"Hey we're men. We need lots of food for our bodies," Shawn said, sticking up for him and Mark.

Once we had our fill, Mark and Shawn told us about their trip.

"We think one of the couples is headed this way," Mark said.

"Why do you think that?" Sam asked.

"Well, when we got to New Mexico, we were able to trace the girl to her adoptive parents. She was found at a gas station right outside of a small town. It was easy to track her after that. After she was found, she was adopted by a couple that was in their mid forties and had no other children."

"We went to their house, but she was no longer there. We pieced together that they were afraid she had gone crazy and took off. Something about her meeting some guy that she claimed she had dreamt about her whole life. They didn't believe her and tried to check her into the psych ward at the hospital. Her adoptive parents didn't seem overly compassionate, and it was clear that they thought she was off her rocker. Once she discovered their plans, she took off with the guy. They seemed almost relieved that she was gone. They did say that she would probably head to California. She had always wanted to move here. She even had a map of California tacked over her bed. It's the only thing she took when she left."

The draw of Santa Cruz obviously had a power over all of us.

"What are their names?" Sam asked.

"Lynn and Robert," Shawn answered.

"Did you get a picture of her?" I asked, curious about what they looked like. "Was the girl Mark's long lost sister? Did she have his warm molasses colored eyes?"

"Unfortunately no, like we said, her parents weren't the friendliest, as a matter of fact, I would say they were downright frigid." Shawn said.

198

"Well, all we can do is wait," Sam piped in. "After all, we wound up here, so if their half as smart as us, they will too."

We decided to hang out at my house once we left the pizza parlor. Sam and I wanted to go to our park, but the boys vetoed that. "It was just this morning that both of you were deathly ill. Just because Shawn and I have prince like reviving kisses, doesn't mean you two shouldn't take it easy," Mark said glibly.

He didn't fool us, something was going on. We let it rest though until we were all comfortably situated in my sitting room with bowls of ice cream.

"Okay, out with it. In case you forgot, Krista and I can practically read the emotions of anyone, and we can definitely tell when we're being lied to," Sam said.

Shawn looked at Mark, who shrugged his shoulders. "We may as well tell them, they need to be on the lookout anyway," Mark said.

"We noticed on the way to the airport before we left, that someone was following us. We tried to pull over a couple of times to get a look at the driver, but every time we did, the car would speed by us. Neither one of us got a good enough look, but we could tell that it was a guy. It just doesn't seem like a good idea to be walking around a park at night," Mark explained.

"Who do you think it is?" Sam asked intrigued.

"We don't know, like I said, we couldn't get a good look at the driver," Mark answered.

"Are you sure it wasn't your imagination?" I asked. "We were pretty stressed out after my mom freaked out on us."

"Maybe, I just think we should all be a little more cautious for the next few days," Mark answered.

"Hey, let's change the subject. I don't want to ruin the good mood. Why don't we play a game?" Shawn suggested.

We agreed we didn't want to ruin the mood, just when things seemed to be normal again. We pushed it to the side and decided to ignore it for at least the night.

I got up and turned on some music and got out our monopoly game.

The mood began to lighten up again as Sam kept us laughing at her usual antics. She took the game lightly and thought it was funny every time she landed in jail. She was generous with her money and kept giving it away. When one of us would buy a property that was the same color as hers, she would give us hers. Shawn kept telling her she had the game backwards.

"You're supposed to accumulate property not give it away," he would tell her every time she gave one away. She laughed and told him that was the way she played the game.

We finally gave up on the game when Sam ran out of assets and money. I put the game away, and we lounged around chatting until my mom came up to tell us it was bedtime.

Sam and I grudgingly walked the guys down to the porch and said our goodbyes; we weren't looking forward to the separation. I felt a little panicked that my emotional health would regress again, once Mark wasn't with me. Sensing my unease, he gave me a searing kiss before he left.

"I will see you in the morning," he said quietly, not bothering to mention that we probably wouldn't see each other in our dreams tonight.

I didn't try to hide my despair. I could control the emotions, but I was still sad over my loss.

Now that Mark was unemployed, he and Shawn were going to continue their research, trying to locate the others. Shawn had given the Boardwalk his notice; we all felt for the time being that our time should be dedicated to the search. Mark told Shawn he could crash at his house and save money that way. They planned on spending part of their morning watching the Boardwalk on the off chance that Lynn and Robert were there.

Sam and I talked long into the night. Not about the disturbing stuff, like the strange guy that might be stalking us, or the twist my dreams had taken, but about the love stuff. We joked about my talk with my mom, and Sam died laughing as I told her the trick I played on Mark. Sam then filled me in on how her walk went with Shawn.

"We talked about marriage," she confessed.

"You did?" I asked surprised.

"After the way the separation made us feel, we decided we never want to go through that ever again. He didn't officially ask. We just talked about it. You know how it is, we made comments like, 'when we get married we'll do such and such thing.' Don't you and Mark do the same thing?" Sam asked.

I thought about it. I did assume that we would eventually get married; we just hadn't talked about it yet. It all seemed so sudden. It was funny to think about how fast things were moving. A week and half ago, I had no friends and no boyfriend. Now, I had the very best friend, and I had thoughts of marriage swirling around in my head. I shook my head at the irony of it all.

True to his word, Mark and Shawn were on my doorstop thirty minutes before school started the next morning. I threw myself in Mark's arms the instant I swung the front door open. I felt no shame for my exuberant reaction when he crushed me to him. The loss of our dreams seemed more pungent this morning. We gave no notice when Sam and Shawn gave us privacy and headed for Mark's Navigator.

"I missed you so much," I murmured into his neck.

"Me too," he said, leaning in to kiss my lips one last time. I wound my arms around his neck and deepened the kiss. I couldn't tell if the ache that filled me was a normal teenager hormonal ache, or just another side effect of the loss of our dreams.

"I better drive you to school before you're late," he said, ending the kiss.

I sighed in disappointment.

I yelled good-bye to my mom who was already in her art studio.

The guys filled us in on their plans for the day on the short drive to school. The plan was for them to hang out at the

Boardwalk for a while on the off chance that Lynn and Robert showed up. We knew it was unlikely, but we hoped they would run into the other two. After that, they planned on spending the rest of their time on the internet searching for clues on the last two.

Sam and I were envious that the guys would be doing something productive while we were stuck at school. We were tempted to skip, but knew my mom would freak if she found out. We were going to have to toe the line for awhile if we hoped to stay out of trouble.

The guys promised to be back as soon as school let out and then we would all head back to the Boardwalk before it turned dark and continue our mock stakeout.

Sam and I were both quick to notice that once again we seemed to be the center of attention. Obviously, our pizza appearance the night before had given the gossip hounds new meat to gnaw on.

"Looks like you two are quite popular this morning," Shawn commented wryly.

"I think you should give them something to talk about," Sam said.

"You mean like this?" I said, suddenly feeling mischievous; I looped my arms around Mark's neck and planted my lips on his.

I meant it as a joke, but once I started kissing him, my lighthearted mood disappeared and I was lost in the kiss. After twelve hours apart, my body craved his touch. Finally, just a little breathless, I broke the kiss.

203

"That'll show them," Shawn said, chuckling. Sam joined in.

"I guess I went a little overboard," I said, just a little bit embarrassed. God, when had I become so brave?

"It was just right," Mark said, dropping another light kiss on my lips.

Shawn and Sam said their goodbyes. They tried to outdo our kiss, but Sam was attacked by a case of the giggles, which ruined the effect.

Sam and I were still giggling when we headed up the stairs toward our homeroom class. We found our seats and were chatting away as the room began to fill. We both felt lighthearted and were in high spirits.

"Are you feeling better?" a voice asked from behind us.

Looking up, we were surprised to see that one of the gossip hounds was actually talking to us.

"Much," Sam replied, turning away thinking the conversation was over.

"That was a cute guy you were with last night. Have you known him long?" she asked nonchalantly.

Of course, she was only talking to us because she had seen us out with the guys. She was trying to fish for information that she could pass along to all her cronies. They were all the same; they were only interested in getting all the dirt.

"My whole life," Sam quipped, dismissing the girl by turning back to me.

She stood behind us for a few seconds more. I could tell she was shocked that we hadn't bowed down because she had shown us some attention. She walked off in a huff. Sam let out a snort of laughter as we watched her retreating back.

It was much the same the whole day. Everyone was suddenly interested in Sam and me. More people talked to me that day than all the other days I had been at school put together. The only one who had nothing to say was Matt, though I caught him watching me throughout the day.

The attention of all the other students got old fast and I regretted going to the pizza place the night before. For someone who preferred to fade in the background, I felt like I had a spotlight pointed at me the entire day.

Finally, the last bell of the day rang; Sam and I exchanged a look of relief. The stares had sapped all the cheerfulness out of Sam's normal demeanor.

"I feel like I've been in a fish bowl the whole day," she said, sounding annoyed.

I agreed with her. I hoped that this new popularity would wear off soon. I didn't know how many more days I could put up with all the attention and mocking glances.

Mark and Shawn were waiting for us on the front stairs. Their day hadn't gone the way they had planned either. They had lost track of time at the Boardwalk.

"So, we didn't get any research done," Mark explained to us apologetically.

"How did you lose track of time at the Boardwalk?" I asked curious.

They looked sheepish. "Um, you lose track of time when you go into the arcade and blow through fifty bucks worth of change," Shawn muttered.

"Oh, so you get to go play games all day while were in school?" Sam said in mock anger.

They stumbled over themselves to come up with excuses. "We would have left sooner, but Shawn kept challenging me to rematches of Galaga," Mark said, trying to defend himself.

We burst out laughing. "I was just kidding," Sam said. "We don't expect you to be working all the time."

"What a way to sell me out though," Shawn said, throwing a fake punch at Mark.

So the day wasn't a complete loss, we decided to scrap our plans of heading back to the Boardwalk and go to my house instead to surf the web.

My mom came out of her studio as we all stampeded into the house.

"Is it okay if we do some research up in my sitting room?" I asked.

"Sure, I'm finishing up my project. Why don't you guy's grab a snack and I'll grab a couple buckets of chicken later for dinner. I'm assuming all of you want to eat dinner together?"

"That would be great," we all seemed to say in unison.

"But I can go get it," Mark volunteered.

"That's okay. I have a couple of other errands to run anyway," she said as she headed back to her studio.

Mark and I grabbed chips and salsa while Sam and Shawn grabbed sodas for everyone. I snagged a handful of wrapped chocolates out of the dish on the counter on our way out of the kitchen. Mark smiled when he saw me pocketing the candies.

I shrugged my shoulders. "I don't get my candy fix at school anymore. I have to take the chocolate where I can get it," I said.

We spent the afternoon searching the web. It was tedious work to go from one site to the next. Without knowing where the last two kids had been abandoned, it was like looking for a needle in a haystack.

The afternoon slipped away and soon my mom called up the stairs to tell us that she was on her way out. We continued to search for a while longer and I soon got sick of following endless rabbit trails that led to nothing. I switched off the computer feeling a little frustrated.

I stood up and turned on the stereo. I cranked the volume up when I heard the new Katy Perry song playing.

Mark pulled me to my feet and took me in his arms. You couldn't call what we were doing dancing, but more like swaying to the music. Whatever it was, it was enough for me. I loved every moment that I was in his arms. I knew that it was important that we find the others, but at times I wished we could be like any other ordinary couple. I rested my head on his shoulder as we danced to the music.

I forgot and lost all meaning of time until my phone rang.

I looked at my watch as I searched for the phone. My mom had been gone a long time, where was she? I found the phone under the Lazy Boy. It stopped ringing by the time I reached it. I checked the caller ID and saw a number I didn't recognize. I punched the number in and waited for someone to pick up on the other end.

"Memorial Hospital how can I direct your call?" A chipper voice asked.

I felt a sinking feeling "I'm not sure, I just missed a call from this number."

"Do you know anyone who may be at the hospital?" the voice asked.

Had something happened to my mom? "Um, can you look up the name Cindy Miller?" I asked as my heart sank.

"Hold please."

Mark came up behind me and set his hands on my shoulders. I looked up to see Mark and Shawn standing by me while Sam turned the music down.

The voice came back on the line. "A Cindy Miller was just brought in an hour ago. She's in the ICU."

I thanked her and hung up the phone.

Before the emotions could attack me and incapacitate me, I held my breath and smothered them out before they could even start. I was not going to get sick when my mom needed me.

"My mom was in an accident, we need to get to the hospital now."

Sam grabbed our purses and we all barreled down the stairs.

Mark reached for my hand as he drove. I was grateful for his touch, the breathing technique helped, but his touch kept my emotions from getting out of control. The drive was silent as the others sensed that I needed the time to think.

Mark pulled up in front of the emergency room. Sam and I jumped out while Mark and Shawn went to park the car.

I hurried toward the admissions desk.

"My mom was brought in a little while ago, can you tell me where I can find her?" I asked with a small quiver in my voice.

"Her name dear?" The woman asked.

"Cindy Miller."

The women typed her name in the computer and scrolled down.

"She's in the ICU, which is on the second floor. If you follow the signs it will lead you up there," she said handing Sam and I a badge.

I thanked her and turned to Sam. Sam knew what I needed. "I'll wait here for the guys. You go check on your mom. We'll meet there."

I walked down the hall and took the elevator up to the second floor. I felt a strange sense of déjà- vu. I was reminded of when my mom and I had made a similar journey when we arrived at the hospital after my dad's heart attack. I felt the emotions approach, but once again I fought them back, at least I was getting stronger at doing that.

I showed my badge to the woman at the desk in the ICU. She typed my mom's name into the computer.

"Okay dear, your mom is being checked over by her doctors right now, as soon as they know something they will come out to see you. You can wait in the ICU waiting lounge which is two doors down on the left."

"Thanks," I mumbled heading out the door.

The ICU lounge was empty except for one elderly woman who sat in the corner silently crying while she shredded a tissue in her wrinkled hands. She wore a flowered housedress and bright pink Crocs. Her gray hair was gathered at the nape of her neck in a tight bun. I felt instantly bad for her and wanted to offer some kind of comfort, but I felt my own sanity was hanging by a thread.

Mark, Shawn, and Sam found me five minutes later sitting on the edge of one of the cushioned seats.

"They haven't told me anything," I said before they could ask. "The doctor is supposed to come out when they're done with her."

Mark and Sam sat at my sides holding my hands. Shawn paced back and forth while we waited. If I wasn't so anxious I would have been touched at his brotherly attitude.

The waiting room door opened and we all looked up to see a harassed looking doctor enter. "Ms. Miller?" He asked glancing at Sam and me.

"That's me," I said standing up. Mark and Sam followed lending their silent support.

"Your mom was brought in at approximately 7:20 pm, tonight with multiple injuries. She is in surgery right now; we had to rush her in to remove her spleen. Our best surgeon is with her now. She broke her leg and multiple ribs on the left side of her body. One of the jagged edges of the rib bone pierced her spleen, which is why we had to remove it. She also suffered a concussion and was unconscious when she was brought in. As soon as we know more we will let you know," he said, edging out the door before I could even get a word in.

"Wait," I said.

He paused in the doorway. "How did it happen?"

"We heard it was a hit and run. Whoever hit her rammed into the driver's side and then fled the scene. The police will be in soon to talk to you," he said sympathetically as he left the room.

I sunk into the seat and felt my emotions beginning to take over.

"Krista, don't let them do it," I heard Sam say from far off.

The waves were building momentum.

"Mark you have to help her. She needs to be here for her mom."

"Krista, you have to fight it," Sam begged me as Mark rained kisses all over my face and rubbed my back.

I swallowed back bile as I fought with the nausea and focused my breathing. The roaring of the waves in my ears was painful. I can't do it, I thought helplessly.

"You can do it," Sam said as if she could read my inner turmoil. She tightly gripped my hand as Mark continued to sooth me.

Mark finally took matters into his own hands and leaned in to kiss me on the lips.

I tried to pull back; I didn't want to make matters worse by being sick all over us.

211

Mark was having none of that running his hand up firmly behind my head and fastened his lips on mine. The effect was instantaneous, like the lull before a storm, yet the storm seemed to be gone as his kiss worked its magic throughout my body. Who needed breathing tricks when you had kisses like this?

My eyes fluttered open as Mark pulled back. He looked smug and knew that his kiss had worked.

"Well that worked," Sam muttered dryly next to me.

Shawn stifled a chuckle.

I felt my senses returning, I may not have stopped it the way I was supposed to, but we had fought the storm together and won. I felt slightly off. Instead of the lethargic feeling I was used to, I felt oddly strong like I was riding an adrenaline wave. I looked around and would have chuckled at the old woman's face if it were different circumstance. I could only guess at what she was thinking about the way we seemed to handle our grief.

"I'm better," I said meeting the concerned eyes of my friends. "I'm worried about my mom, but I feel much better," I continued quietly keeping my voice down.

We were interrupted when two policemen walked into the room. Neither of them could give us any new information. It seemed like no one had seen anything. The only lead they had was the paint scrapings on the side of my mom's focus.

I thanked them for their help and sat back down when they left.

"I'm going to stay here at the hospital tonight."

"I'm staying with you," Mark said putting his arm around me.

"I can stay too," Sam said.

"No, there's no need for all of us to stay, but you and Shawn can crash at my house," Mark told her. "Maybe you can stop off at Krista's and pick up a change of clothes for her."

"Can you feed my cat too?" I asked.

Sam and Shawn hugged me goodbye and headed out. I was amazed when I looked at my watch and discovered it was almost midnight. I felt bad that Mark was stuck in a waiting room all night, but I was grateful to have him with me.

The doctor came in shortly after 1:00 am and told me that my mom had made it through the surgery okay and was resting now. She still hadn't regained consciousness, but he said rest was the best thing for her body right now anyway.

Mark and I moved to the loveseat in the corner. I snuggled against his side while we watched infomercials on the television that was mounted on the wall. We had the lounge to ourselves. The elderly woman was picked up by her family shortly after Sam and Shawn left. We talked for awhile until I drifted off.

I woke the next morning with a kink in my back and a stiff neck. Mark and the Boardwalk were once again absent from my dreams, but at least I had gotten a little sleep. I missed the dreams, but had more pressing matters on my mind. I was anxious to see my mom and hoped she regained consciousness today.

Mark was still dozing when I sat up straight. I rubbed the back of my neck to help work out the kink and then stood up, my back groaned from the new position. I went searching for a bathroom. I took a mock sponge bath in the sink and scrubbed the last traces of sleep from my face. By the time I made it back to the waiting room with two steaming cups of hot chocolate, Mark was up and alert.

"I was just on my way to look for you."

"Sorry, I felt so grimy I decided to wash up a little. Here, I brought you a hot chocolate, the breakfast of champions," I said with a small smile.

Sensing my stress, Mark led me back to the loveseat and draped his arm around me while we watched television. We sat quietly sipping our hot chocolate. His presence once again offered the comfort I needed. When our cups were empty, Mark stood up and tossed them in the recyclable bin.

"I'm going to go check on my mom," I said standing. "The waiting is killing me."

Mark snagged my wrist as I was heading out the door. He pulled me gently in his arms and wrapped his hand around the nape of my neck securing it into place. He leaned in and gave me a kiss that would rival the one from the previous night. The warmth of the kiss spread through every limb in my body and made my toes curl in anticipation. I knew I should be worried about morning breath, but I couldn't seem to be able to pull up one ounce of embarrassment.

Mark pulled back and I took a small stumbling step backward as all my other senses came back into focus.

"Um, Ms. Miller," An aggravated voice said behind me. I flushed slightly turning around to face my mom's doctor. I could tell by his expression that it was not the first time he had called my name. I can just imagine what he was thinking. I was some shallow teenager who makes out in a waiting room while her mom is laid up in the hospital.

Instead of being embarrassed, I felt a small surge of anger inside. He had no idea what I have to deal with and he definitely didn't spend the night on a small uncomfortable sofa.

"Yes," I said in a defiant voice.

"How is my mom?" I continued on in a softer voice that could not disguise the pain I felt over my mom.

His expression softened at my apparent concern. "She's better. She is still in a coma, but that is partly due to the medicine we're giving her. The less she moves as her injuries heal the better chance she will have of recovering. We're going to be moving her out of ICU and into a regular room later today. We need to run a number of tests on her this morning, so why don't you go a home for a little while and get some rest."

"Can't I see her now?" I asked in a pleading voice.

"She's having a CT done now and after that we're going to do an MRI. Come back after 3:00, she will be in a room and visiting hours are lot more lenient," he said leaving the room.

"He's right, let's go home and get refreshed. That way if your mom does wake up, she won't stress because you look worn out."

215

"It's too early to call Sam and Shawn to come get us," I said glancing at my watch, trying to come up with a valid reason to stay.

"They dropped the car off last night after you fell asleep. Shawn didn't feel comfortable leaving us stranded. Come on, we will go home for a little while and be back before you know it; I promise," he said, gently leading me toward the bank of elevators.

I followed along reluctantly, glancing back at the double doors to the ICU ward one last time before the heavy elevator doors closed.

Shawn had parked Mark's SUV on the second level in the parking garage. Mark was helping me into the vehicle when an industrial van with tinted windows pulled up behind his car.

The passenger door opened and a distinguished gentleman stepped out. He looked vaguely familiar and I tried to place him.

"Dad, what are you doing here?" Mark asked beside me, clearly confused.

At his words, it came to me how I knew him. He was much younger in the picture that I had seen, but I could now clearly tell it was him under the wrinkles and gray hair. I turned to look at Mark questioningly who was also confused and saw a hulking shape coming up behind Mark.

I opened my mouth to scream, but no sound came out as I felt a sharp pain on the back of my head. I was out before my head hit the ground, and never saw the person who delivered the blow that knocked me unconscious.

Chapter 12

I woke slowly with my head pounding, feeling very disoriented. It was pitch black in my room as I opened my eyes. I reached over to turn on my bedroom lamp, but felt nothing but open space. Where was my lamp?

And then it all came flooding back to me. My mom in the hospital and Mark's dad showing up in the parking garage, but I didn't remember anything after that.

I abruptly sat up. Where was Mark?

My sudden movements only accentuated the painful throbbing, like someone was hitting my head with a hammer.

"Mark," I said quietly, feeling around with my hands. "Mark," I said much louder, starting to feel panicked. I climbed off the cot I was laying on, dropping to my knees. "Mark!" I said again, my voice rising to a near scream.

I crawled around on my knees, holding my hands in front of me like a blind person. "Mark. Where are you?" I said choking on a sob. I continued to reach out my hands, finding nothing but cold hard wall. The darkness was beginning to taunt me as the sobs ripped out of me. I crawled back over to the cot and curled up into a ball.

I tried as hard as I could to stay calm, but the panic was beginning to overwhelm me. I closed my eyes and began holding my breath. *Smother it out,* I chanted in my head, *smother it out.* The room felt like it was spinning, leaving me groggy. Unable to keep my eyes open, I drifted back to sleep.

The second time I woke was less confusing as I expected the oppressive darkness when I opened my eyes.

I hoped my eyes would adjust to the darkness, but it was no use. There was not even the slightest bit of light to help.

I lay on the cot for a few minutes, trying to figure out why this was happening to us, and why Mark's dad was involved.

"Mark," I said trying one more time to see if he was with me, but there was no answer.

I cautiously sat up and was relieved that my head at least felt a little better. I swung my legs off the edge of the cot and stood up. Reaching my hands out, I took a cautious step forward encountering the rough bricks of a wall. I trailed my hands along the wall trying to get a feel of the room and its dimensions. It felt like it was about the size of my bathroom at home, minus the fixtures.

There was only one door which seemed to be bolted on the outside. The only fixture in the room was the cot I had awakened on.

I sat back down on the cot trying to control my senses. I had lost all sense of time and could not tell if it was day or night. I focused, trying to use my heart as a gauge. It was just beginning to ache, so I knew that meant I had been away from Mark roughly four to six hours. I wonder what Sam and Shawn could be thinking?

None of this made any sense. Why would Mark's dad kidnap us? If only I could remember more of the details before I had blacked out.

Other questions of more concern pressed on me.

Where was Mark, and what had they done to him? What about my mom? What if she woke up and I wasn't there?

My head began to ache again, so I lay back down to deal with the pain. The endless darkness made it difficult not to feel tired, especially lying there with my eyes closed.

Suddenly, I could hear the lock on the door being disengaged. Light flooded the room followed by the door being pushed open.

Blinking in the sudden brightness, I looked up to see a heavy duty florescent light above the cot. It was making a faint buzzing noise and was flickering like the bulb needed to be tightened. I stared at it blankly for a moment while my eyes adjusted.

After a few seconds I was finally able to focus clearly. I looked around at my surroundings and wrinkled my nose in disgust at what I saw. The walls were painted a dingy white and were covered in scuff marks and stains; I didn't even want to speculate about what had caused them. I saw the door I had discovered in the corner of the room, it was in bad shape like the walls. It was made of steel that had once been painted, but was now peeling in multiple areas. I finished my scan of the room and was right about my earlier estimate of its size. It was roughly 6 feet by 8 feet.

A woman I had never seen before walked into the room carrying a tray, followed by a large burley man. The woman set the tray on the edge of the cot. There was some food and a bottle of water, but it also held several needles.

"Arm," the woman said.

"What?" I asked.

"Arm," The woman repeated. "I need give you this shot," the woman said impatiently. "Either you can let me do it or Bruno can help convince you," she said, nodding over at the man who was still blocking the doorway.

I didn't feel like being held down against my will, so I didn't fight as the woman tightened an elastic band around my arm. It pulled at the fine hairs on my arm, causing me to wince, but she paid no mind. She tapped the skin on the inner side of my elbow trying to coax a vein to the surface. I felt the prick of the needle as it found the vein and watched as she proceeded to inject me with several vials of a thick liquid. I cringed at the thought of them pumping something foreign into my body.

"It's nice to see you so cooperative; your boyfriend could stand to be more like you."

My head jerked up. "Mark, where do you have him? You have to let me see him! We have to be together." My words tumbled out of me in a rush. The mention of Mark had made my heart start racing. "Please you have to let me see him, I need to be with him," I pleaded.

221

"We know you need to see him. Why do you think we have you separated?" she said as she gathered her empty vials and headed out the door.

I heard the lock being engaged after the door was closed. What did she mean, that's why they have us separated? Did they know that I got violently ill when he wasn't around?

I was so frustrated that I grabbed the tray and chucked it against the door.

The metal tray hit the door with a dull thud, sending the food flying, but the water bottle bounced harmlessly off the wall.

"Well that did a lot of good," I said to myself.

I needed to think.

It was now obvious that they wanted to do testing on us. Why else would they be injecting my arm with some unknown fluid? They also seem to know exactly what they were doing to us by keeping us separated.

The lights flickered off as suddenly as they had flickered on.

The sudden darkness made me uncomfortable again. I've never confided it to anyone else, but I have always been secretly afraid of the dark, and this was the worst kind because I didn't know my surroundings that well.

I curled back up into a ball tucking my head under my arm. The effects of being separated from Mark were beginning to intensify, causing a dull ache throughout my body.

I tried to take my mind off of the darkness by thinking about sections from my favorite books. This helped slightly; making the darkness easier to bear.

As I lay there, I let my thoughts drift thinking about Shawn and Sam.

Had they realized that something happened to us? Would they come looking for us? Mark's car was still in the parking garage. I just hoped they wouldn't say anything to my mom if she woke up. If she knew I was missing she would freak out, and that wouldn't help her recovery.

My throat was definitely dry from thirst. I had been trying to ignore it, but it only intensified. Especially, since I knew that there was a bottle of water somewhere on the floor. I didn't want to give them the satisfaction of drinking their water or eating their food, but after awhile I began to realize I was only hurting myself.

I got down on the floor and felt around trying to locate the bottle of water. I found the wrapped sandwich they brought me and after a few more minutes, I also located the water bottle. It had rolled under the cot after I pitched the tray at the door.

Settling back on the cot, I twisted the cap off the bottle and gulped the water to sooth my parched throat. I screwed the cap back on and picked up the sandwich. I paused before my first bite to take a sniff, it smelt like turkey. I took a small cautious bite, it tasted wonderful and I inhaled the entire sandwich before I knew it. I guess I didn't realize how hungry I was. I knew I should save the rest of the water, but the sandwich was a little dry. I twisted off the cap and only sipped enough to wet my throat again, then recapped it making sure the lid was on securely.

The darkness of the room and a full stomach began to make me sleepy again. I laid down tucking the water up by my chest so I wouldn't lose it, and in a few minutes I was out.

The lights woke me up.

I sat up and looked around, but nothing had changed. I just wished that I could see Mark. I missed him so much and needed to be with him.

The lock was released on the door and this time I was surprised to see Mr. Russo, Mark's dad, accompanied by Bruno.

"Why are you doing this to us?" I asked sadly, "He's your son."

"Doing what?" he answered, not acknowledging the second part of my statement.

"Holding us against our will," I said.

"I wouldn't worry your pretty head about that now," he stated in a condescending voice. "You're insignificant in the whole scheme of things anyway."

I felt hatred begin to well up inside me.

"What do you mean, insignificant?" I asked incredulous.

"You'll find out soon enough."

"You have to let me see Mark. I have to be with him."

He waved off my questions like I was an annoying gnat, bothering him.

"Enough talking, you will find out all the answers to your questions in due time. I want you to be clear on exactly what you are before I'm done with you."

"Bruno, perhaps you can escort the lady now," he said as he walked out the door.

I ignored Bruno's hand and stood up on my own. They may be treating me like a prisoner, but I would be damned if I will let them haul me around like one.

We walked down a narrow hallway, passing several closed doors. At each one, I tried to pause to see if I could hear Mark behind any of them.

Finally, the hallway opened up to a large room that looked like a big oversized garage, big enough to house airplanes. The ceiling was a least 30' high and the space itself could hold my entire house. Off to one side, I saw a row of at least ten computers. A couple of lab tables sat side by side next to the computers with about two feet of space separating them. On the other side of the massive room were microscopes and other equipment I could not make out. One looked like an x-ray machine, with another lab table under it.

Several people milled around the room, but none acknowledged my presence.

The woman who had given me the shots earlier was standing against the wall talking to another person. Finally, there was another intimidating looking man that could have been Bruno's twin. He had the same beefy build, but his hair was just a shade darker.

Looking around, I was filled with despair. I had been harboring the idea that I could somehow elude them and escape, but it became clear there was no way we were getting out of here.

Bruno took my elbow and escorted me to a door that was off to the right of the building.

"Bathroom," he said shortly obviously not a man of many words.

I turned the knob and walked in. The small bathroom offered no means of escape, it was windowless and the ceiling seemed to be made of a solid single sheet of metal. It held a metal toilet in the corner and a metal sink by the door. I looked around for a few moments getting a feel of the space. Sighing in frustration after a few minutes, I gave up seeing no way to escape. I sat on the toilet and relieved my full bladder. When I was done, I washed my hands at the sink and took a moment to splash water on my face.

I heard a knock on the door; apparently I had used up my allotted time.

I opened the door finding Bruno waiting for me. "They want you by the machine over there."

He obviously didn't know what all of the machines were either.

"Why?" I asked.

"I don't know. I don't get paid to ask questions."

I scanned the room with my eyes trying to file away as much of the set up as I could. Except for the hallway that I had been escorted through, the only other door into the lab was the door that led to the bathroom. I at least now knew that there was only one way to get in and out of the lab.

I approached what I thought was an X-ray machine, but upon arrival, could tell it was like no other I had ever seen. It looked like most of the occupants of the room were readying the equipment. One was fiddling with a computer that was hooked up to the machine, while another adjusted the placement of the lab table underneath. The rest just stood there watching me approach.

"Sit on the table please," Russo told me. I refused to think of him as Mark's dad.

I sat on the table as they proceeded to attach wires to my collar bone and temples. They assisted me on lying down so that the wires wouldn't pull free. Two of the assistants pulled arm restraints out and tried to attach them to my wrist. I pulled my arms back.

"No," I said, near panic now. What could they possibly be doing to me that they needed to strap me down?

"Don't be difficult. This test will be as hard as you make it. If you fight, it will only get worse."

I shook my head no. With a sigh, Russo beckoned Bruno and his look alike over.

I sighed, reluctantly holding my arms out. The techs strapped them securely to the boards and then moved to my ankles. I wanted to protest, but knew it would do no good. Once they had my ankles securely attached, they moved up to my head and strapped it down to the board.

The straps cut painfully into my wrist and ankles.

227

"These hurt," I said, but no one responded. "These hurt!" I said, louder this time.

"They're not supposed to be comfortable, now be quiet."

I laid there trying to hear what they were discussing.

"Is the other subject ready?" Russo asked. I figured he was talking about Mark, but I couldn't believe he was referring to him as a subject. It seemed hard to believe that he shared the same DNA as Mark.

"Yes, we had to knock him out to get him into the containment room, but the camera is up and ready to record."

"All right then, let's get started. You need to make sure the sequence is right," I heard an unfamiliar voice say.

Sequence? I thought, beginning to panic. *What the heck did they have planned for me?*

"Amanda, check the sensors on her temples."

"Yes Mr. Russo," Amanda said formally as if addressing an official. I could practically feel the hero worship emitting from her.

She carefully inspected each sensor as the other spectators stationed themselves on the far side of the machine where the control panel was.

I tried to turn my head to watch them, but the strap holding my head in place kept them just out of my line of vision. I heard Amanda tell someone else to grab more sensors for my heart.

A few seconds later, the neckline of my shirt was pulled down as another sensor was attached.

I could only lie there, helplessly waiting for what was about to happen. My pulse began to quicken and I could feel my hands begin to shake. I tried my breathing technique to steady them, but the claustrophobic feeling of being tied down was more than I could handle.

"Okay, we're ready to go," said someone off to my right.

Before I could brace myself, a stabbing pain radiated through my forearm where one of the sensors rested. I screamed out in pain.

"Oh no, that won't do," Russo said, walking back to the front of the table where I was strapped down. I felt a moment of relief thinking that maybe he wasn't a monster after all.

"Amanda, bring me the mouth restraint," he said undoing my head strap.

I felt my panic rise as she approached with some kind of medieval face mask. I shook my head from side to side as they tried to strap the mask around my face. Bruno was beckoned over to hold me steady, wrapping his massive hands around my head as a single tear trickled down my cheek.

"Please, don't do this," I tried to plea, but no sound came out.

"Very good, no need for all of us to hear your screams," he said walking away as Amanda re-strapped my head to the table.

This time I tried to brace myself for the pain, but it came from another sensor unexpectedly. I bucked against the table as a knife-like pain slashed through my other arm.

229

Sobbing, I tried to plea with them, but my words never made it past the mask. The next pain was below my collarbone and was more staggering than before. Each jolt seemed to intensify every time they shocked me. Over and over again in different locations, they tortured my body.

I lost all track of time and my vision began to blur. I yearned for my emotions to take over, anything to help me escape what I was suffering.

I began to hallucinate and could see Mark off to the side. Though he wasn't strapped down, he seemed to be in greater pain than I was. I wanted to reach out to him, but my arms were too heavy, I could no longer feel them attached to my body.

"Mark!" I tried to cry out. I could read his lips as he called out my name and then there was darkness as I mercifully passed out.

I came to suddenly, finding myself in a wheelchair under a steaming shower. I was still fully dressed and my clothes were soaked through.

My throat burned and tasted of bile. I looked down and discovered that I had vomited all over myself.

I felt someone behind me as they squirted something in their hands and scrubbed my hair. I could feel their frustration as they roughly scrubbed my head.

The water abruptly turned off. I was instantly chilled from the soaked clothing against my body. My teeth began to chatter uncontrollably.

"James, you can't leave her sitting in the cold like that," I heard Bruno say through the noise of my chattering teeth.

I felt the straps being undone.

"Look man, they didn't tell me when they hired me I was going to have to clean puke off some girl."

"Yeah I know, but it's not the girls fault. You heard her screams. She was in some serious pain. I don't think I will ever forget the scream she made when they first turned on whatever that machine was," Bruno said. As he finished taking off the bindings, I felt a warm blanket being tucked around me and surprisingly gentle hands under my knees picking me up out of the chair.

I was weak as a newborn kitten as he carried me down the maze of hallways. I kept my eyes closed, but tried to gather my thoughts. They had obviously carried me into a different part of the building to bathe me because the hallway we had taken earlier was a straight shot without any turns.

Finally, I heard a door being opened and I felt myself being lowered onto a cot. I opened my eyes although I was extremely dizzy, and could see that I was back in my room. Bruno was standing in the doorway. His clone James was holding a folded stack of hospital scrubs and a couple more blankets. He set them on the cot without a word. Bruno shot me a look of what looked like sympathy, but it could have been just a trick of light.

I heard the lock reengage. I sat up slowly and was surprised at how weak I was. I used my arm to steady myself and cringed when I saw the ugly mark the sensor had left.

231

Steadying myself didn't work, so I laid back down trying to catch my breath.

The lights flickered out.

"Go figure," I muttered.

My teeth stared to chatter as a shiver ran down my body. My wet clothes had soaked through the blanket that was wrapped around me. I knew I needed to get them off. I used the last of my strength to shimmy out of my wet jeans. It took several moments to recover from the exertion and by the time I started on my shirt, my teeth were knocking painfully against each other. My shivering was so intense that the cot began to shake. It took some work, but I managed to shrug out of my shirt, and slip on the scrubs that were sitting on the edge of the cot. I was so exhausted I barely had the strength left to tuck the blankets around myself.

This time though, my sleep was not dreamless.

The dream started the same as every other dream I had ever had. The Boardwalk in the distance and soft rolling waves washing up on shore. I felt extremely relieved to be here at our spot again. There was a light breeze off the ocean that left a slight chill in the air. My eye was caught by the sudden movement of someone running across the beach toward me. It was Mark. I rushed to meet him and just as he was about to reach out to me, his hands encountered some sort of barrier, stopping him in his tracks. I reached out with my hands, feeling the strange force field that was keeping us apart. It was invisible to the naked eye, but it didn't make it any less impenetrable.

"Krista, are you okay?" I heard him ask. I was shocked. We had never been able to talk before in the dreams and even though there was an invisible wall separating us, I could hear him clearly.

"I'm scared."

"I know you are, but don't worry, I'm going to find a way out."

"What if you're too late? I can feel myself getting weaker with each passing minute."

"I won't lose you. I am going to get us out of this situation; you just have to be strong."

I placed my hands on the invisible barrier. Mark placed his palms to mine. I could not feel them, but the memory of his touch made it feel almost real.

The feeling was lost as I felt my body being tugged from the barrier by some unseen force. Mark was being pulled in the opposite direction. I could see him fighting it as he tried to grab onto anything and everything. Finally in desperation, I heard him call out his love for me.

I began to weep as the distance between us grew. I tried to tell him I loved him also, but I was being dragged out of my dream.

I blinked at the sudden light that filled the room. I was disappointed that the dream had not eased the ache in my heart, instead realizing that I was feeling sicker than before. At this point, I guessed we had been separated for more than 24 hours now.

I tried to raise my head but, laid back down acknowledging the fact that my strength was sapping away. Maybe my violent bout of sickness had escalated it, but I was getting worse by the moment.

My musing was interrupted as the door to my room was opened.

"They want to see you back in the laboratory," Bruno said stepping into the room.

I sighed and tried to sit up, my body fell weakly back down to the cot. Bruno reached down and with one hand and pulled me to my feet. I tried to steady my balance, but my water like legs made the effort useless. They gave out from under me, but before I could hit the floor Bruno scooped me back up in his arms.

I was grateful for his help, but could not express it as I laid my head against his arm and closed my eyes as he carried me out of the room.

I dozed off for a moment during the walk down the hall, but was awakened by the many voices and activity in the room when we entered.

"I don't think she can handle another round of whatever you did to her last night," I heard Bruno say. "She was too weak to even hold her head up."

"Yes, the testing can be quite rigorous, but when the others join us, it will be well worth it. We have to see how far she can be pushed," Russo said.

"I just feel tha..."

"I'm not paying you to feel, or think for that matter! Just do your job and leave the thinking to me, understand!"

I tried to make sense of anything that I was hearing. Push me for what? I thought. Could he really be responsible for my dreams? What about Sam and Shawn?

"Why are you doing this?" I asked in as strong a voice as I could muster, not wanting to give them the satisfaction of knowing how weak I really was.

"Why? Because, it's the most logical way to test my theories."

I looked at him in dismay. He was still talking in riddles.

Noting my confusion, he sighed.

"Well, I did promise you some answers, and it's obvious you don't have much longer. Though I am quite disappointed that my experiment failed, I expected the injection to have a stronger effect at this point, but I shouldn't be surprised. You women have always been weak. It's a wonder we didn't die out centuries ago," he said disdainfully.

"Where to begin," he started. "I guess the best place is the beginning."

"In the beginning..."

Was he kidding? It sounds like he was quoting the bible.

"There were many of us through the years and we all converged here in Santa Cruz."

"Why?" I asked trying to process both his statements.

He looked at me like I was a disobedient child for interrupting him.

I clamped my mouth closed not out of respect, but sensing he would stop talking if I didn't act like the puppet he wanted me to be.

"We are drawn here because Santa Cruz is what you would call *Holy Ground.*"

"What do you mean *Holy Ground*?" I asked.

"Can I continue or are you going to act like an insolent child?" He asked in the condescending tone I was beginning to hate with a passion.

"*Holy Ground*, meaning that celestial beings are drawn here, or more accurately, *Guides* and *Protectors* are drawn here."

My head reeled at his words. 'Celestial Beings?' 'Guides and Protectors?' My religious background was sketchy, but I did know that 'celestial beings' meant angels or something like that, but I had no idea what he meant by 'Protectors' and 'Guides.' A million questions raced through my head, but I held my tongue.

"In fact, Santa Cruz means *Holy Cross*," he continued. "For centuries, our kind gathered here and were then dispersed by arch angels to go out and ward off the evil that plagued the earth," he said with bitterness dripping from his voice. "We were paired with *soul mates*, creating a predetermined connection between a Guide and a Protector. Plus, our reproduction ensured that our kind would continue from one generation to the next. "The Guides," he said looking at me bitterly, "were created to use their emotions to find the evil that lurked in the human spirit and use that emotional power to try to sway them to the *good side*, instead of the path they were on. Protectors were sent to protect the Guides at all cost. The trick is that one cannot survive without the other. I'm sure *they* felt we would cherish the bond that tied us together. I, however, was the exception. I survived the loss of my weaker companion and became stronger despite the severing of our bond. I plan on making the remaining Protectors like me. Meaning, the life of a Protector will no longer rely on that of a weak companion that is susceptible to every human emotion. So you see my dear, I will fix God's mistake. Of course, I had hoped that the injection I gave you would make you stronger; giving you better control over your emotions, but science sometimes takes time doesn't it? Unfortunately for you however, time is a luxury you no longer have. I'm sure your death will destroy your Protector, just as every other Guide's death has before you."

His hatred was tangible.

I wanted to know what had happened to the rest of the Guides and Protectors, but was suddenly more scared of him than I had ever been. His dark, evil aura surrounded him making me feel extremely uncomfortable.

"It was easy to destroy them you know," he said, picking the thoughts out of my head; I knew instantly that Sam and I had been right. We could read each other's minds; we just needed to master it. I shook my head. I would not play his games.

He snorted once again, rummaging through my head. "Oh come now, you wanted the truth after all. It wasn't I that

237

created our kind this way, but it will be me that fixes it," he said, sounding almost proud of himself.

His egotistical confession was horrifying. How many had he murdered? My heart constricted as I thought of my parents, so casually tossed to the side. Grief threatened to overtake me as I thought of all the lives lost. *Was he a...* I searched for a phrase I remembered hearing years ago in my one attempt at attending church when I was younger.

"Fallen Angel?" He said impatiently rummaging through my head. "Your ignorance is almost overwhelming. You're supposed to be more superior to typical humans, but you seem to lack the IQ I am used to dealing with."

Like I cared at this point what he thought of me. I did wonder though, if we were directed by angels, how he was able to murder innocent people without any repercussions?

"I have the protection of another higher power, you could say; one that encourages my talents," he said with a sinister smile that made my skin crawl.

"Why were we abandoned? Why not destroy all of us? We were practically babies," I asked angrier than I had ever been. He had destroyed all our lives and seemed so pleased by his deeds.

"My intention was never to destroy our kind, but to make it stronger. Your parents wouldn't listen to my ideas, choosing instead to trust in a creator that made them weak. They left me no alternative but to eliminate them. I have been watching and observing all of you for the last fifteen years. I know everything about all of you. It was only a matter of time before you were drawn here, just as we were before you. Soon, the other Protectors and Guides will come as well, feeling the call of the Holy Cross. Let me rephrase that. The others will join me since you and your significant other will no longer exist."

An errant thought hit me. "Don't you mean the other four? There's still another couple out there besides Lynn and Robert."

"Once again your assumptions are wrong. I never said I gave up all of you. I kept the more docile pair as my own. They adore their papa and would do anything for me. They've been raised to appreciate how special they are. Through my guidance, they have become more powerful than even I could have imagined. The girl shows none of the weakness you exhibit, and soon I will have all the information I need to complete my work.

"Don't look so dismayed my dear. It is all for the greater good. The others will become stronger because of your sacrifice."

"You're a monster," I said, not afraid of his anger.

Surprisingly he was not angry, instead he laughed.

"A monster? I don't think so. I just took back some of the power. There was a flaw in our DNA makeup when we were created and I decided to fix it."

This was all sickening, I thought. *Where did such evil come from?*

"They will stop you," I told him.

"On the contrary, I believe they will look at your deaths as a lesson. In fact, they will embrace me as a father. They have felt lost throughout the years, just as you have, but I will help them realize how special they are and how strong they can become."

I knew he was wrong, and I felt bad for the others. Soon they would have to face this monster also. Mostly I felt sad for Mark and me. We would never have children, and we would never grow old together. He was stripping our lives away from us just like he had with our parents.

"No more questions?" he asked in a mocking voice.

I was silent. There was nothing else to ask. He was the monster I had imagined him to be. I would give him no more satisfaction.

"Well, I see the last part was a deal breaker," he said with a small laugh. "Think of your part in this as furthering the lives of the others. I think we can continue with the experiments now," he said as he turned and walked away.

I wanted to protest, to plead with him not to hurt me anymore, but I didn't want to give him the satisfaction. I remained silent as they strapped me down to the same table as before, remaining rigid as they fastened my ankles down. Only when the woman approached with the dreaded sensors did I finally respond. A silent tear rolled down my face. I looked around as best I could with my head strapped down and saw everyone busy at various computers, only Bruno was watching me.

The sensors were placed in different locations this time and I eyed them with renewed panic remembering the pain they caused before.

The first jolt sent a flash of fire through my body.

I was too weak to scream like I had the day before, but I did let out a slight moan. The next round was more severe than the previous jolt and I welcomed the darkness as I once again lost consciousness.

When I woke, I was not in my cell. I was still in the laboratory, but someone had moved me to a different table. I wasn't wet this time, but my hair was damp so once again they must have bathed me. Looking around, I could see that the laboratory was nearly empty with only one grunt over by the computers. I looked around for Bruno, but he was nowhere to be found. I wondered briefly how Russo had managed to get so many others to help him, but I guess evil wasn't hard to find in the world.

I closed my eyes; at least they hadn't locked me back in the cell. Maybe they realized I was no longer a threat. I knew the end was close. My guess is that we had been missing for over thirty-six hours now. I had a small nagging feeling that there was something I had wanted to do, but I was too tired to focus on what it could have been.

I continued to lie there, feeling like I was drifting in and out of consciousness.

The next time I opened my eyes there was a considerable amount of activity going on throughout the lab. Several of the people I had seen the last few days were huddled around one of the television monitors.

"Look at him. His strength it is out of this world." One of them commented. "Mr. Russo was right, her pain makes him stronger. It's a good thing that door is steel plated. It's too bad he's missing this. Where did you say he disappeared to, Amanda?"

"I didn't, it's no concern of yours what he chooses to do with his time," Amanda said in a brittle voice.

I tried shifting to better hear their conversation, hoping that no one would notice and reattach my restraints.

Luckily, no one even looked my way. I was apparently nothing but a lab rat; something insignificant to experiment on and then dispose of. I knew that would come sooner than later.

I started to close my eyes again, but then I finally remembered a previous idea I had forgotten; Mr. Russo's ability to read my thoughts. Could Mark and I do the same with each other?

I gnawed on this new bit of information. If telepathy was a possibility could I reach Mark and try help save him at least?

I felt it was at least worth a shot.

I closed my eyes to concentrate, fighting the urge to drift off to sleep, which is what my battered and weakened body now craved.

Now was the time to be strong. *Concentrate*, I chanted to myself.

Mark, I thought. *I know this is crazy, but answer me if you hear this.*

I tried again, *Mark, please answer me if you can hear this.* I repeated it over and over again, to no avail. I didn't want to give up, but the many hours of being separated from him had just taken too great a toll on me. I've never experienced the ache that I was feeling now. As I worked to keep my mind focused, I could hear footsteps approaching the table.

Amanda stood over me, attaching more sensors for yet another round of torture.

I had no strength left to protest, instead only to lie and accept my fate. Strangely though, I felt nothing but soft vibrations. Was this the end? Maybe I was too far gone to even feel the pain anymore.

My thoughts began to dissipate and I slowly drifted off.

This time Mark was already waiting on the beach for me. My heart sped up as I spotted him. I struggled toward him, but the lethargic feeling had followed me into the dream. I reached the still invisible wall that separated us to see Mark looking at me in horror. He raised his hand as if to touch my face.

I watched as his concern was replaced with anger. His fist clenched and struck the wall sending invisible ripples vibrating up from the ground.

I stepped closer and placed my hand on the barrier to comfort him. His frustration was evident by his heavy chested breathing. He placed his hand to mine on the barrier and looked into my eyes.

Not knowing how much time we would have together, I tried to tell Mark everything that had happened; the truth about his dad, about our parent's death, the others, and about 'Guides' and 'Protectors.' It was a lot of information to take in.

"Plus, I think it's possible for us to read each other's minds," I said, finally winding down from my longwinded speech.

"Why do you think that?" he asked.

"Because your dad was able to read mine, I just don't know how he did it yet."

"I think the key is to open our minds..." my voice trailed off as the wall separating us evaporated.

"How did you do that?" Mark asked in amazement.

"I told you, I think that we are all connected through our minds. I haven't pieced it all together, but I am slowly beginning to figure all kinds of things out."

I looked at our hands that were now touching.

Our fingers were intertwined and I relished the familiar heat of his touch. I reached up and softly stroked his face as he kissed the middle of my palm. In the next instant I was pulled strongly into his arms. The ache that had followed me into the dream loosened, just by the touch of his embrace. I sighed as he put his hands on my waist and pulled me close for a heartbreaking kiss. I clung to his shoulders, molding my lips firmly to his; I could feel his warmth spreading throughout my body. I moved my hands up to his head greedily taking what he was offering. The ache eased and as I pulled away, I could feel the air feeding my hungry lungs.

His soothing touch gave me instant relief, at least here in the dream.

Mark pulled me down to sit on the sand with him. He tugged on my hand and settled me between his jean clad legs, wrapping his arms around me, pulling me tightly against his hard chest. I rested back against him as he took one of my hands into his.

"I have missed you so much," he said. "It's been impossible to control my rage, plus they've told me nothing."

"Well just before I fell asleep, they were discussing your strength increases. It seems the more pain they inflict on me the stronger you become."

Mark tensed at my words. I forgot I had glossed over the shock treatments on my earlier explanation.

"What do you mean they inflict pain on you?"

"They've been shocking me with jolts of electricity, obviously testing to see how far your strength will go. Your dad wants to see how far we can be pushed. He survived your mom's death and I think that's his ultimate goal for the other Protectors. His real problem is the fact that the Protector's life depends on someone he thinks is weak," I said trying to clarify the source of Russo's madness.

"I just can't believe my father is capable of this kind of evil."

I grabbed his hands and twined my fingers through his. "Neither did the others," I said.

I kept expecting to be ripped away from him at any moment.

He obviously felt the same, because as the time passed, he wrapped his arms more firmly around me as if anchoring himself to my body. I had a more pressing thought on my mind, but was trying to avoid bringing it up.

"Are going to get out of this alive?" I asked softly.

Mark made no comment at first. I angled my head so I could look up at him to see what he was thinking. He leaned forward and brushed a brief kiss on my lips. "I don't know," he said a breath away from me. He leaned down and pressed his lips more urgently to mine.

My heart broke into a million pieces. This could be the last time we would see each other. I felt a hot tear burn its way down my cheek. Mark stroked it away with the pad of his thumb. We did not talk again and when I woke I could still feel the heat of his touch.

I opened my eyes and looked around to find the lab was once again deserted. I scanned the room as my eyes adjusted to the dim light. Sitting up, I expected to be too weak to move, but I felt surprisingly alert. My body still ached, but the feeling of heaviness had receded.

I lay back on the table as I heard someone enter the lab. It obviously wouldn't be good for me if they found out I had regained some of my strength, another round of torture would be brutal. I couldn't help wondering though if maybe it was the injection Russo had given me that had me feeling a little stronger.

I remained as still as possible quietly listening to the movements of the person who had entered the lab. I heard the rapping of computer keys and then the shuffle of feet as they moved from one computer to the next. A few moments later I heard the familiar tapping of Amanda's heels on the polished cement floor. I was worried that Russo would arrive considering he would be able to pick through my mind and know that I wasn't as weak as I appeared, hopefully he was still away from the lab like I had heard the previous night.

I kept my eyes closed realizing this made my other senses stronger. I could smell the coffee in the machine across the room as it began to drip in the waiting pot below and the overpowering perfume that clung to Amanda in a nauseating way. It wasn't just my nose that seemed stronger; my ears were picking up many noises around the room, like the impatient tapping of a woman's fingernails as she waited for the coffee to finish brewing.

Finally, I heard the sound of multiple feet as they entered the room. Amanda passed out daily instructions, which led me to believe that Russo was indeed gone for the day. I kept my eyes firmly closed and willed my body to remain lifeless as someone raised my arm to check my pulse. I remained spaghetti-like allowing my arm to hit the table with a heavy thud when they finished. My cover was nearly blown when a cold metal stethoscope was pressed to my chest causing me to wince slightly. Thankfully the worker was too preoccupied with another conversation to notice. After a few moments the stethoscope was removed and I could feel a blood pressure cup being applied to my upper right arm, with a few pumps the band constricted tightly around my arm. Once completed, I heard the scratch of a pen on paper as the person jotted down my statistics.

"Her stats are still running high, but her body seems to be depleted of all strength. She remained unconscious through the simple exam, I believe she doesn't have much longer," the voice said.

I lay there, quietly contemplating what I should do next. They were obviously waiting for me to pass away. How long would they wait before they decided to take matters into their own hands? I knew I would have to act the next time they left me alone, if my strength remained.

The lab was noisy with activity as everyone worked at their stations. I passed the time by trying to connect to Mark, but no matter how hard I concentrated I was not able to make my mind respond the way it needed to. I could feel that I was close, but I didn't know how to bridge the gap. Every few hours someone would come over and go through the routine of taking my stats. Each time I would will my body to remain limp. I was amazed that I continued to get stronger as the morning progressed. I soon felt that if I wanted to, I was capable of movement. I believe that the time I spent with Mark in the dream had made me much stronger. Lying on the table for so long though, I became acutely aware of the fact that my body was dehydrated and my stomach was empty. The thirst I could ignore, but I laid there in fear that my stomach would betray my half dead state. I played mind games in my head trying to remain alert, wanting to be sharp incase I had to move quickly.

Finally, when I thought I would go stir crazy from lying on the table for hours, I heard someone say it was lunch time. There was steady noise throughout the room as everyone closed up their stations and headed to lunch. The room slowly emptied and was soon quite, but I remained still and decided to wait a few moments before I moved.

My heart almost stopped when I heard someone approach my table. I laid there, barely breathing feeling the person's eyes on me. I kept my eyes closed and tried to even out my breathing.

After what seemed like an eternity, the person finally walked away. I forced myself to wait a few more minutes before I dared to open my eyes.

I blinked in the light as my eyes adjusted to being open. I was definitely alone. This was the opportunity I needed; I was going find Mark and get us out of this mess.

I sat up and was taken aback by how lightheaded I felt; I needed to find food fast. After a few moments to clear my foggy head, I swung myself off the table and stood on shaky legs using the table for balance. My first steps were tentative as my body betrayed my determination, but I made my way to the coffee pot where I found leftover muffins.

The pot was empty, but I was pleased to see a left over muffin in the basket. I grabbed it quickly and gulped it down. It was dry from sitting out unwrapped all morning and the last bite got stuck in my already dry throat. I scanned the room and my eyes lit up when I spotted a half filled bottle of water sitting at one of the work stations.

The water helped the last of the muffin go down and I felt better with something in my stomach.

There was another bottle of water at the last work station. I picked it up and curiously glanced at the computer screen to see Mark locked in a cell similar to the one I had occupied. I moved the mouse hoping to enlarge the screen and was surprised when a different room came into view. The room was definitely not in this building. The rich exterior and massive size of the room made me think of a ballroom you would find in a mansion on television. The room was richly decorated, but that was not what grabbed my attention.

The image showed two individuals reclining on leather sofas that sat in the far corner of the massive room reading. Could they be the missing pair that Russo raised as his own children? I stared at them for a few minutes wondering what their fate would be. Finally, I dragged myself from the screen; getting out of here was more important now.

I cautiously headed down the hallway, pausing at each door to listen for any signs of the goons that were holding us hostage. If it was silent, I would try the door knob. The first one I tried was locked. I made a mental note that Mark might be locked in there and moved on to the next one, but it was locked also.

"Crap," I said, quietly moving on. The next three were also locked. Finally, trying the fifth door, the knob turned. I opened the door and recognized the room I had spent the first thirty six or so hours locked-up in. Moving on, I tried the next door which also opened when I turned the knob. The room appeared to be a supply closet. I gave the room a quick once over and then shut the door. I finally hit the end of the hallway which split off in two directions. I was just about to go right when I heard footsteps.

I quickly darted back the way I had come; I ducked into the supply room, and closed the door softly. I pressed my ear against the door and listened to the footsteps as they passed by. Another set followed closely behind with another behind them. I could hear their conversations as my captors headed back to the lab.

I waited. I knew I needed to get out of the supply room before they discovered I was missing. My hand was on the door knob and I was starting to turn it when I heard several more sets of footsteps.

I released a hiss of air. That was a close one.

I waited a few more seconds then turned the knob; I stepped out of the room and looked in both directions. The coast was clear. I took off down the hallway as the adrenaline raced through my veins propelling me forward. I hit the fork in the hallway and turned to the right, running at a pace that was unfamiliar to me. It was as if my feet had been given a boost, they propelled me full force down the hallway. Before all of this, I would have said my body was using my adrenaline as energy, but I now believed a higher force was helping me.

The long hallway ended with a door. I twisted the knob cautiously and stepped out of the hallway into the room. It was another room like the lab except it was occupied by a small Cessna plane. I had been right when I thought the lab looked like an aircraft hangar. I rushed across the large space and headed out the door that had an exit sign lit up over it.

I made it, I thought stepping out into the brilliant sunlight. Now I needed to locate a phone and call Shawn and Sam. I would need their help if I was going to help Mark.

I looked back with a pang. I hated to walk even a step further away from Mark, but I knew I must if I was going to save him.

I rushed around the side of the hangar and stopped dead in my tracks.

I had found Bruno.

Chapter 13

Bruno was leaning against a white Ford F-150 smoking a cigarette. He dropped the cigarette when he spotted me. I made eye contact with him and saw him jerk his head slightly toward the direction I had just come.

I backed away slowly and gave him a small smile of thanks. Once I was back around the corner, I headed in the opposite direction. I took off at a fast trot and rounded the next set of aircraft hangars and spotted an airport office up ahead. I marveled when once again I was able to run at a pace that would have made a track star's jaw drop. I reached the door and opened it slowly. I cautiously walked into the small space, finding the office was empty.

I closed the door behind me and franticly searched for a phone. My heart raced when I spotted a dirty white clunky phone on the corner of the desk. I picked up the receiver and went weak with relief when I heard the dial tone.

I punched in Sam's cell phone with clumsy fingers. The phone rang and was picked up instantly.

"We're sorry the number you dialed is not in service, please check the number and try again," a recorded voice said.

My heart sank.

I tried again. This time I took my time and the number went through. The phone rang twice before it was answered on the other end.

"Hello," Sam said.

I could have wept with joy at the sound of Sam's voice.

"Sam, it's me."

"Krista? Thank God, we have been worried sick! Where are you?" Sam said in a rush.

"We were kidnapped! I need your help, they still have Mark locked up," I told her urgently.

"Where are you?" Sam asked.

"At some aircraft ha..." My words were cut off as the phone went dead.

Dread filled my whole body, but it was easy to fight it back. For the first time in my life, I was in charge of my emotions. I turned and faced the door bracing my hands on the desk behind me. As the knob was turning, I felt the cool metal of some kind of tool where my left hand had landed. I slid the tool into the waistband of my scrubs just as the door swung open.

Bruno's almost twin James was standing in the doorway. I tried to back away from his grasp, but the desk stopped my backward motion.

James seized my arm and dragged me out of the office. With his other hand he dragged a radio out of his pocket.

Pressing the buttons, he paused. "I got her she was trying to make a call, but I cut the lines just in time."

"Take her to her mate. We will be taking care of them tonight. I'm done with these games," Amanda said on the other end.

James grabbed me by my arm and started to drag me back in the direction I had just escaped from. Though they had found me, I felt a rush of excitement from Amanda's words. She told him to take me to Mark, in a few moments I would see him. It had been over forty eight hours since I had last seen him in the flesh, and not in a dream state.

I kept my eyes open, observing my surroundings as James continued to drag me back into the building. I was soon in the familiar hallway where my own cell was located. James walked a few more doors down and paused at the first door I had tried earlier during my flight down the hall.

He paused and used his free hand to pull a gun out of the waistband of his pants.

I gasped when I saw it. I had seen guns before on T.V, or on a policeman's belt, but I had never been this close to one.

James pointed the gun at me and told me not to move as he released me so he could unlock the door. Once the door was unlocked, he told me to open it. I twisted the knob at the same time that James pushed me through the door. He kept the gun pointed at my head.

"Don't move or I'll shoot her," he said as he backed out of the door.

My eyes met Mark's as James backed up out of the door. Mark looked ready to spring, but stayed put when he spotted the gun pointed at my head. James cleared the doorway and slammed the door behind him, engaging the lock.

Mark rushed over to my side and dragged me into his arms. He buried his face in my hair and ran his hands over my arms and down my back looking for injuries.

"Are you okay?" he asked anxiously.

"Yes, I'm fine, believe it or not, except for sores from the sensors, I feel kind of great."

Mark pulled back slightly, looking confused.

"You do look good. I have been so worried about you. We've been here for over forty eight hours. I expected you to be as ill as you were where when your mom kept us apart."

"I was, but last night in the dream when the wall disappeared, I felt a lot of the sickness leave me. At first I thought the feeling would disappear when I woke, but it didn't, in fact I started to regain all of the strength I had lost. We did something in the dream. I think it happened when I talked about us opening our minds. It's like we opened a locked cabinet, we took control over our dreams. I think if we survive this, we will not be pulled apart anymore. It was like our dreams were trying to give us a warning that something bad was going to happen to us."

"You mean that our dreams somehow saw the future?" Mark asked skeptically.

I laughed at his tone. "You're going to doubt that when all of this has happened? We defy the norm on everything. I have found out so much in the last two days. Like the fact that some kind of celestial beings sent us here to protect humanity. Dreams that could tell us our future seemed like small potatoes in comparison."

Mark looked at me, intrigued.

I became self-conscious with him looking at me like that.

"What?" I said.

"You seem almost energized like you're riding high or almost happy about something, you're glowing. You look absolutely beautiful."

I assessed his words, he was right, I did feel energized. Maybe it could be left over from the adrenaline rush from earlier, but even though we were locked up and facing a threat, I felt oddly happy, almost like everything was okay.

"I think it's *because* I'm with you. Even though I know we probably won't make it through the night, I'm okay with it as long as I am with you. It's only when I'm away from you that I feel so lost. The only thing that would make this better is if I had a chocolate candy bar," I said playfully.

Mark smiled at my comment.

He pulled me even tighter into his arms; it would have been painful if it didn't feel so right. I felt him brush a kiss across the top of my head. "I'm glad you're with me too."

I looked around the room for the first time and laughed. Mark must have had many fits of rage. The bed, which was no longer sitting normal, had countless restraints still hanging off it. It looked more like it had been tossed in a trash compactor.

The metal was bent at odd angles that made it look more like a jungle gym than a cot.

"Rearranging your room?" I asked with another giggle in my voice.

Mark smiled slightly embarrassed. "That's why James pointed the gun at your head. They don't trust me; he thought I would rush him even with him holding a gun. They have tried to weaken me, but the more time that passes, the more frequent the rage comes on. I think I scare them," he said with a smile as he bent the metal of the bed as close as he could back to its original position.

I sat on the edge of the now rickety bed as he held my hand. I filled him in on my morning excursion; making it outside of the building and discovering that we were being held at some kind of storage hangar for airplanes. I then told him about finding the phone, but being cut off before I could tell Sam more about our location.

"I'm proud of you, but I can't believe you put yourself in that kind of danger, you should have fled as soon as you hit daylight."

I looked at him with disbelief. "You think I would have left without you? I told you before, I can't live without you. Would you have left me?"

"That's different. I'm the guy, it's my job to protect you, and in case you missed it, I'm doing a lousy job of it. You're out there trying to find a way out for us while I sit in here cooling my heels," he said with barely controlled frustration.

I placed my hands on his chest to neutralize his anger. "We may only have a few hours left. I don't want to spend them in anger and frustration. I want us to make the most of our time together," I said in a pleading voice.

Mark rested his hands on top of mine. I could feel the heat of his body. I felt a light blush approach as I thought of how alone we were. I was suddenly filled with the feeling of wanting to be with him as much as I could be. I had always said I would wait until marriage, but what if they did kill us tonight. We would never discover the true feeling of being together in the fullest sense.

I looked up and could see the same thoughts mirrored in his eyes as he reached the same conclusion as me. He leaned forward and placed his warm lips on mine. It was like being lost in the desert and finding an oasis waiting for you. I locked my arms around his neck and pulled him closer. Drinking greedily, I took everything his kiss had to offer. I felt more in tune with him than ever before. I opened my mind finally finding the key and our thoughts merged. The kiss deepened and without even realizing it I was lying down with Mark sprawled on top of me. My lips parted as he deepened the kiss even further. My thoughts were wrapped around Mark's as we discovered the joy of each other's lips. We had never kissed this intensely. I saw his desire in his thoughts mirrored my own.

Mark left my lips and found his way to my neck. I leaned my head back as his lips found the pulse in my neck.

"I hate to break-up the love fest," a snide voice said behind us.

It took us a few moments to return from the place we had journeyed to with the kiss. Finally, we realized we were no longer alone. Mark pulled back and looked behind him. I looked over his shoulder and saw James standing in the doorway.

I should have been embarrassed that he caught us in such a compromising position, but I didn't. Instead, I felt disappointed that we were interrupted. I knew I told my mom I wanted to wait, but that was before all of this. Besides, half the girls in my old school had already done it numerous times; I was one of the few that had waited. This was probably the last time we would ever be together and we had been interrupted.

My mind picked up Mark's thoughts and I saw that he was disappointed also. How ironic that we had figured out how to read each other's thoughts when it was too late.

"Get up," James said, pointing the gun at us.

I sat forward and felt something dig into my back. The screwdriver, I had forgotten about it. I spent half a second trying to figure out how to send the signal to Mark until I realized he already knew. I felt his hand slide into the back of my pants and dip below the waistband.

"I don't want to distract you," James said pointing the gun at us.

By the time we were on our feet, Mark had successfully stashed the screwdriver in his pocket. His pants were baggy enough with oversized pockets, that the screwdriver was almost completely concealed.

James kept the gun pointed at my head. He was smart enough to know that Mark would not risk my life that way. We shuffled out the door and made our way down the rest of the hallway and into the lab.

Amanda was in the corner with Mark's dad.

Mark paused, willing his dad to look our way. If he was reading our thoughts he gave no indication. I couldn't help wondering if he would still destroy us. Hadn't we given him what he had strived for? We had shown him we could become stronger.

He approached us as Mark and I passed our thoughts back and forth.

Focus. We have to block him out, I thought to Mark.

The connection was unlike anything I had felt before. I could feel Russo inside my head, probing my thoughts. I concentrated as hard as I could to push him out and could tell by his expression that it was working.

"Impressive, both of you. It's a shame I can't trust you enough to let you live. You may have indeed been useful."

He snarled as my smile turned to dread. I guess that answered my previous thought. We were now just a liability.

"Get on the tables please. My time with you is finished," he said waving a hand toward James as if to get his point across.

Mark made a half movement to step in front of me, but James pressed the gun to my head to stress the point that they still held the upper hand.

Mark looked indecisive.

Should we try to fight? His thoughts flashed in my mind as he ran the scenario through his head. He was strong, but there were just too many of them.

"Don't even think about it, I won't hesitate to put a bullet in her head," James said as if he understood what Mark was contemplating.

Mark approached the table and looked back at me. It seemed crazy to give up without a fight, but he could not bear watching James carry out his threat.

I looked at Mark and could see his body tensing as his thoughts filtered through my mind. I knew he was ready to make his move when a grim smile flashed across his face.

If we were wrong we would be shot, but if we didn't fight, we would die anyway, Mark's thoughts hit my mind.

I simply nodded my head slightly in agreement as Mark palmed the screwdriver that was hidden in his pocket.

My own body tensed waiting for Mark's signal.

When I move, run. I can take them on if I don't have to worry about them harming you. You are more delicate than me. Just run! Mark's thoughts filtered through my head.

I trained my eyes on Mark, waiting for him to make the first move.

In one swift movement Mark plunged the screwdriver into James's leg, dropping him to his knees. Mark did not pause. He took his fist and rocked James on the head, sending him falling backwards to the floor.

I watched in horror as the gun in James' hand went off.

My blood roared in my ear as I watched Mark crumble to the floor. Darkness threatened to engulf me, but I fought it back. Mark needed me. I rushed to his side and laid my hand on his face, willing him with my mind to respond.

I sobbed as I felt hands dragging me away from the only person who made me whole.

I felt the room begin to spin as my insides caved in. I didn't even see the waves of emotions come on as they no longer held any meaning. The spinning of the room took over and I welcomed the blackness with open arms. My life had lost all meaning.

I was pulled out of my blissful darkness by a loud crash.

I turned my head toward the noise and was surprised to see a vehicle barreling toward me. I tried to move out of the way, but realized I was tied down.

My eyes began to focus as several things happened at once. The vehicle screeched to a stop inches from me as the individuals that surrounded my bed began to scatter. I was surprised that they were wearing surgical garb.

My mind tried to wrap around everything that was going on, it was like I was watching a movie from a distance. I looked around in horror as I discovered that the masked goons were interrupted just as they were going to start hacking into me.

The crack of gun shots echoed in the room as James shot at the van, shattering the windshield into a thousand pieces.

The driver of the van stepped out of the vehicle holding a gun in his hand. He used the open door as a shield for his body. I was surprised to see that it was Bruno.

"I called the police and they're on their way..." His words were cut off by a new wave of gun fire.

He returned the gun fire, shooting James dead in the chest. He kept firing until his gun was emptied.

Police sirens blared in the distance sending everyone scattering and within seconds the room cleared out.

Russo spotted me in his rush to leave the building; the madness in his eyes was evident. He raised a gun and aimed it at me.

I did nothing to protect myself. I welcomed whatever he wanted to do. I was disappointed when he lowered the gun and fled from the room. I turned and saw that Bruno had a gun pointed where he had stood.

Bruno rushed to my side and didn't bother undoing the restraints he simply pulled a deadly looking knife out of his boot and cut the straps. He threw me in the van and I landed on the floor of the van in a heap. I had no idea what he was going to do with me nor did I care. I closed my eyes and tried to block out all thoughts of Mark. I could no longer feel my heart. It had broken into a million pieces and was gone.

Suddenly I was startled as something heavy landed on my right leg. I opened my eyes as Bruno threw the van in reverse and tore out of the warehouse. I could hear the sirens in the background getting louder, but as Bruno drove away they became a distant sound.

My eyes finally focused on the heavy weight on my legs. I gasped when I saw that it was Mark. Bruno had grabbed him before we fled from the building.

I cried at the sight of Mark's body. Why would Bruno do this to me? I could not bear to look at Mark's lifeless body.

"He's still alive," Bruno told me. "I felt a faint pulse before I grabbed him."

I pulled my legs out from under Mark and kneeled at his side. I put my shaky fingertips to his neck and wept with joy when I felt the faint pulse under my fingers.

My hands became frantic as I searched for Mark's wound. I pulled up his shirt that was soaked in his blood and found the wound. Darkness threatened to pull me under when I saw the blood flowing out of the wound but, I fought it back.

He needed me and I was not going to let anything get in the way of that.

I shook my head to clear my thoughts and looked around franticly for something to staunch the bleeding. The van held the same equipment that had been in the lab. My scan of the interior told me there was nothing in the van that would help Mark.

I did the only thing I could think of, placing my hand over the wound to try and stop the steady flow. His warm blood ran between my fingers. I cried silent tears as I felt his pulse growing weaker.

"Please hurry," I pleaded to Bruno in a broken voice. "He's slipping away," I said with a broken sob.

"The hospital's right up the road," he said.

I felt relief at his words as he began to slow the van down. I looked up thinking we were at the hospital, but to my dismay we were parked on the side of the road.

Bruno jumped out and jogged around the vehicle and opened the door.

"Why are we stopping? We have to hurry he's dying!" I yelled at him in a hoarse voice.

Bruno stripped off his shirt and pushed it under my hands that were still pressed over Mark's wound.

"I can't take you the rest of the way, there will be too many questions. Drive the rest of the way, its right up the road. Tell the doctors that you were walking on the beach when some thugs jumped out and robbed you and shot your boyfriend."

I looked at him in confusion.

"I don't know if any of this talk about angels is true, but you didn't deserve any of this," he said as he turned to run away.

"Wait!" I yelled. I threw my arms around him and gave him a quick hug. "Thank you."

I watched him for a brief moment as he jogged away and then adrenaline took over. I raced to the driver's side and threw myself into the driver's seat. I slammed the vehicle into gear and flew down the road. I hit the hospital parking lot going ninety and did not stop until I reached the emergency room.

I tore into the E.R. yelling that my boyfriend had been shot and was dying in my car. Several doctors rushed after me as I raced back to Mark.

Within moments they had him on a stretcher and had started C.P.R. I watched as they searched for a pulse. I fought to hold onto his hand and begged them to save him as they raced him into the hospital.

I felt a nurse tugging on my arm trying to pry me away from him, but I fought her off. I was not letting him go. I knew that as long as I continued to touch him, he wouldn't die.

I felt the sharp pain of a needle being plunged into my throat. I felt my hand slip away from Mark's and tried to call out, but it was too late. I didn't get a chance to tell them how important it was for them to save him. That I could not survive without him.

I knew I was dreaming. I was sitting on the soft sand that I had sat on hundreds of times before. I looked around for Mark, but saw him nowhere. I sat and watched the waves approaching and the birds flying throughout the sky. It was actually quite peaceful. There was a slight breeze that carried the scent of the amusement park in the distance. Just when I was about ready to give up, I saw him approaching. I was surprised to see that he was not alone. Four others stood behind him.

I recognized Sam and Shawn and thought one of the other couples looked familiar too, but couldn't place them.

Mark stopped in front of me and held out his hand to me.

I stood up and faced him. "Are you dead?" I asked him.

"I don't know. This isn't my dream, it's yours."

I looked at him in horror. What did he mean this wasn't his dream? We had always shared the same dream.

My screams echoed throughout my body and I felt like all of the air was leaving my lungs.

Chapter 14

I was awakened by my own choking as I gasped for air. I sat up abruptly on the hospital bed I was laying on and looked around frantically for Mark.

I felt a gentle hand pushing me back down on the bed and was surprised to see Sam standing over me.

"What are you doing here?" I asked in a hoarse voice. "How did you know I was here?"

"You told a nurse that I was your next of kin and they called me," Sam told me.

I faintly remembered in my drug induced sleep being asked who they should call.

"Where is Mark?" I asked in a pleading voice, dreading the answer.

"He's in recovery," Sam said, wiping the tears off my cheeks.

I thought I misunderstood her.

"He's okay?" I asked, not daring to believe.

"Mark's going to be fine. They say the bullet passed right through him. They went in and fixed the damage it caused, but they said he was lucky that it missed all his vital organs."

"What about my mom?"

"She's getting better; she finally regained consciousness last night, but only for a few minutes. You can go up and see them later when you feel better."

I started to get out of the bed, but Sam laid a restraining hand on my shoulder.

"You have to rest," she told me.

I ignored her and pushed myself off of the bed. I gripped the rail when a moment of dizziness hit me. Closing my eyes, I fought to regain my equilibrium. The dizziness left and I turned to Sam with determination.

"I need to see him; will you take me to him?" I asked with steel in my voice.

Sam looked at me in surprise. She was used to seeing me struggling with my weaknesses, but those days were over. I was no longer weak, and I would no longer be the victim of my emotions.

Sam grabbed my hand and guided me out of the room. We walked past several rooms and stopped in front of the bay of elevators. Sam pushed the up button and the elevator doors opened. She helped me into the elevator and pushed the button for the fourth floor... Sam turned and looked at me. I knew that she had many questions, but I could not answer any of them until I saw Mark.

I had to see with my own eyes that he was okay. Only then would I be able to function again, but until I knew for sure, my body was simply moving on auto pilot.

The elevator doors opened on Mark's floor and we stepped out. Sam led me past a waiting room that had a sign proclaiming it as, *Surgery Waiting Room*. I did not give a single thought to the three other people in the waiting room nor did I acknowledge them as they watched Sam and I walk down the hall.

Sam stopped in front of the nurse's station and told the nurse behind the counter that I was her brother's fiancée and wanted to see him.

I gave her and odd look.

The nurse filled out a pass and handed it to me. I put it on with trembling fingers.

I walked toward his room leaving Sam behind. I paused outside his room with one hand on the doorknob and for the first time since he had been shot, I felt the first stirrings of hope.

I twisted the knob and walked into his room and approached his bed with quiet feet, but stopped when he turned to look at me.

I felt hot tears burn down my cheeks as he gave me a small smile. I muffled a half sob as I rushed to his side.

I reached for his hand and was surprised by his strong grip as he held onto my hand.

"I was so scared you were going to die," I said in a broken voice.

271

"I know. I could hear you. I wanted to answer you, but nothing would work," Mark said in a scratchy voice. "What happened?"

I filled him in on everything that had happened, sugar coating nothing. I told him how I thought he was dead and had wished for death myself. I told him about the gun fight and Bruno saving us. Finally, he knew everything.

He held my hand through it all and his eyes clouded over when I told him about wishing for death. He cringed when he realized how close I had come to being shot and his eyes turned deadly when he heard that his dad tried to shoot me.

"I'm going to stop him," Mark swore in a voice I had never heard him use.

I did not shy away from the suggestion since I had similar thoughts when he had shot Mark. He tried to destroy us and we would not rest until he was stopped.

With all my words spent, I laid my head on his heart while he stroked my hair. I felt all the emptiness in me disappear and soon I began to feel the familiar warmth from his touch spread through my body.

I turned my head and pressed a light kiss to his jaw and heard his murmur of approval. I was just about to trail more kisses along his neck when the door opened.

Two police officers entered the room. One looked to be in his sixties with more gray than brown hair on his head. He had the typical beer belly you expected to see on a cop from the cliché of being doughnut eaters. The second officer was the exact opposite. He was well over six feet tall and was as thin as an anorexic model. He looked only a few years older than me and had the kindest eyes I had ever seen. I felt instantly at ease in his presence.

I sat up straighter as they approached the bed.

"We don't mean to intrude, but we have a few questions about the shooting," the older officer asked.

"Okay," I said, answering for both of us.

"Where did it happen?" He asked as he pulled a notebook out of his pocket.

I plunged into the story that I concocted. That we were walking on the beach when two masked men jumped us and how they grew angry when they discovered I had no purse. They knocked me down and when Mark tried to protect me they shot him.

"They ran away after they shot Mark. I think they thought he was dead," I said in a shaky voice.

"You were very lucky," the younger officer told us as they got up to leave the room.

"One more question?" The older officer said just before they reached the door. "Where did you get the van?"

I felt a moment of panic; I had not thought that far ahead. Suddenly the answer flashed through my head as Mark sent his thoughts to me.

"It was on the road when I helped Mark up off the beach. I know I stole it, but the keys were in the ignition and I felt I had no choice. You can tell the owner I'm sorry," I added knowing they would never find the owner. I knew for a fact that all our captors had vanished.

The cops seemed satisfied and left the room after promising to try to catch the men who shot Mark.

I looked at Mark who returned my grim smile. We knew that the true perpetrators would not be caught; we would have to find them ourselves.

Another knock sounded on the door.

The person at the door knocked again slightly louder.

"Come in," I called.

Sam stepped into the room followed by Shawn and another couple.

I knew who they were instantly. Lynn and Robert had found us.

Sam took over with introductions.

"Krista, Mark, this is Lynn and Robert," Sam said pointing to the couple next to Shawn.

Lynn was taller than me, probably about 5'10." She had dark brown eyes and brown hair that was cropped off in a cute haircut that I would have loved to try, but lacked the guts. She was dressed in jeans that had tears throughout them. They looked like the jeans girls spent hundreds of dollars on, but I could tell the tears were genuine, they were just worn. She wore a black shirt advertising a band I had never heard of. She was quiet and pretty and even though she had more piercings in her ears than most girls I knew, she didn't seem over the top Goth, but more like a person saying, *This is my style if you don't like it too bad.*

Her significant other though was a complete contradiction to her style. His light blonde hair was parted and combed nicely to the side. He had the prettiest shade of green-blue eyes I had ever seen on a guy. He wore chinos that looked like they had been pressed with a half of can of starch. He had a casual polo shirt on, but even that showed signs of being ironed using the other half of the can of starch. He looked like one of the models on the cover of GQ, the only thing missing was a sweater slung over his shoulder.

They seemed as different as day and night, but there was no denying their affection for each other. They were as in sync with each other as a couple that had been married for twenty years.

"So fill us in on what we missed?" Shawn said coming over to give me a one arm hug.

I looked at Mark and he gave a small nod. There would be no story telling for them. They all deserved to hear the truth and to know about the evil waiting for us.

I did most of the talking since Mark had such limited contact with anyone at the lab. I filled them in on everything, about our parent's death, our separation and about the other two that Russo had stashed away. I held nothing back, laying it all out there in the open and watched as the others looked at me in horror as I told them about Mark's dad. I gave Bruno his moment in the spotlight and told them how he saved Mark and me. Finally, I told them about Mark being shot and about my heart breaking when I thought he was dead.

"This was not grief. We can't live without each other, which I already knew since Mr. Russo had filled me in on that part. I felt everything in me die when I thought he was dead," I told them.

It took me over an hour to catch them up to speed. None of them interrupted, they all listened to me with rapt attention. I explained how Sam was right when she suggested that we might share a twin link we just needed to learn to open our minds to it.

"Mark and I were able to do it after he broke down a wall that separated us in our current dreams and figured out how to send thoughts back and forth," I said looking at the others. Sam and Shawn looked shocked, but Lynn and Robert just exchanged a look.

"You can already do it?" I asked them.

"Yeah, we figured it out a few days after we found each other when things got sticky on the road," Lynn said answering for both of them.

"Wow, that's wild," Sam chirped in. "Do you think we can do it with the rest of us too?"

"I think so because Russo had no problem reading my thoughts," I said bitterly.

My last comment broke the silence and soon all of them were peppering me with questions. I answered their questions as best I could. The bigger questions were harder to answer. I didn't know who our arch angel was supposed to be, and I didn't know where the last couple was being held.

The guys quickly got into a discussion about our parent's and our origins while us girls soon lost interest and drifted to the corner of Mark's room. Sam and Lynn caught me up on what I missed while I was held captive.

Lynn was as easy going as Sam with the exception of having a bit of a hard edge about her. I chalked that up to the fact that she had been adopted by people that always wanted to hospitalize her for her abnormalities.

I learned that she and Robert had found each other six months ago while she was on a class trip to Washington. He recognized her instantly, but she thought he was some kook. When he tried to explain that he knew who she was, she quickly ditched him, but that night he stepped out of the shadows in her dreams. When she walked down to the lobby of her hotel the next morning, he was waiting for her. They spent the rest of the trip together. Once she got home though, they rapidly discovered that they couldn't be separated. They tried to explain it to her parent's, but they thought she was crazy and that she needed to be hospitalized.

"We discovered that both of us had the urge to visit here, so we hit the road. We both had already graduated high school, the Washington trip was a special bonus for those of us in the state of New Mexico that graduated early," She added.

My ears perked up at Lynn's last statement. "You were both found in the same state?" I asked.

"No, Robert's dad was transferred there for work. He was found in Texas."

"What do his parent's think about you guys taking off like that," I asked.

"They were fine with it. We stayed with them for a few weeks before we headed this way. They're left over from the hippie days. You know, free love, follow your dreams, which by the way, they completely believed us about the dreams. Of course, I think in their younger days they smoked a lot of pot, so I'm not sure if them believing us was an endorsement or not," she added with a smile.

I returned her smile. Lynn was an easy person to talk to. She had enough of an edge to keep things interesting.

I looked over at Mark and could see he was struggling to stay awake. I shooed the others out of the room and promised to call if anything happened with Mark during the night.

Sam paused to give me a hug at the door.

"Hey, why did the nurse think you were Mark's sister?" I asked.

Sam looked sheepish. "Well are all practically related anyways. Shawn thinks Robert is my brother," she added looking hopeful.

"It's a possibility, both of you share similar features," I said giving her a reassuring hug.

"I am so happy you guys are okay. Shawn and I were so worried; we thought we had lost you both. It really tore Shawn up to think he lost his sister just as he was getting to know you. I felt the same. I was afraid I had lost my best friend," she said tearfully.

I felt bad. I had been so wrapped up in Mark and my drama, I hadn't thought about those we would leave behind. I felt a twinge of guilt for being ready to embrace death when I thought Mark was dead. My poor mom would have been devastated, but I also knew that if the situation arose again, I would still feel the same.

I waited until Mark drifted asleep before I left his room and headed down to check on my mom.

My mom was sleeping when I entered the room. I tiptoed in and sat quietly beside her bed. I reached over and linked my fingers lightly through hers. Her eyelids fluttered open.

"Hi mom," I said choking back tears.

"Hey, honey," she answered in a weak voice. "Are you okay?" She asked, obviously worried about my history in this area.

"I'm fine, just worried about you."

"Don't worry about me; I'm going to be fine," she said in a near whisper, dropping off again.

I spent several hours with her as she drifted in and out of sleep. When the nurse came in to give her pain meds, she suggested I take a break, that my mom would most likely sleep through the night. I thanked her and headed back to Mark's room.

I knew it was probably against hospital policy to stay overnight. The announcement ending visiting hours had sounded a few minutes ago, but I didn't let that deter me. I walked purposefully past the nurse's station and gave a sigh of relief when I saw that the station was empty.

I closed the door to his room softly behind me and headed to the chair beside his bed. I pushed it as close as I could to the bed and lowered the railing of the bed, so I could hold his hand while he slept.

As I watched him sleep, I knew that I would never allow this to happen again. Together we would become stronger. We would never allow ourselves to be the victims again.

Mark opened his eyes a few hours later and saw me watching him.

"You should sleep," he said.

"I'm fine."

Mark used his hand and pressed my head on his heart where I longed to be. I could hear his thoughts as plainly as mine and smiled as I felt his heart beat against my ear. I would never grow tired of listening to his heart. Rightfully, it was my heart also, since neither of us could live without the other. We weren't some aliens or scientific project, we were *meant to be*.

Other great works by Tiffany King:

Forgotten Souls

(The Saving Angels book 2)

The Ascended

(The Saving Angels book 3)